Jellyfish

Jellyfish

Janice Galloway

GRANTA

Granta Publications, 12 Addison Avenue, London W11 4QR

Published in Great Britain by Granta Books, 2019
First published without the stories 'Gold' and 'Peak'
in 2015 by Freight Books, Glasgow

A CIP catalogue record for this book
is available from the British Library.

1 3 5 7 9 10 8 6 4 2

ISBN 978 1 84708 667 9
eISBN 978 1 84708 669 3

Typeset in Palatino by M Rules

Printed and bound by CPI Group (UK) Ltd, Croydon, CR0 4YY

www.granta.com

MIX
Paper from
responsible sources
FSC® C020471

for Jonathan and James and folk who publish,
buy and write short stories

connected and not connected
reflecting an observation by David Lodge:

'Literature is mostly about having sex and not much about having children; life's the other way round.'

contents

jellyfish

A child was dangling over the kerb, the back wheels of his push-chair holding his whole weight, too near the precipice. Water scattered from a passing lorry, sprinkling his jacket-front like glitter. The boy tried to sit up, rocking the buggy, himself within it, over the tarmac abyss. He couldn't be more than two, Monica thought. Maybe less. The rims of the back wheels, his sole contact with *terra firma*, were worn; the chair that held him, thin canvas. A juggernaut rounded the corner, changing gear so the pavement groaned, expecting an avalanche. Monica watched the mother blink, draw her face back from the fumes as the words WASH ME slithered past her, close enough to touch. The boy, however, stayed put, the radiator grille as near as dammit tipping his nose, heat haze rippling his face into strips. The rabbit in his hand shook from the tremor rattling down his arms, his skinny little bones. Then the lorry, its lumbering, unimaginable tonnage, was past. Monica coughed. The exhaust at the kid's eye level. Carbon monoxide. Jesus, she murmured. Holy Mother of God.

Calum tugged her hand. Swearing, he said. He was looking up, little face poker straight. That's a swear. Jesus is only for church reasons.

Sorry, Monica said. She tried a smile, hoping he hadn't seen any of the buggy business, that child dangling like bait. I just thought I saw somebody I knew.

Who? he said.

Jesus. I thought I saw Jesus and I was just saying hello. So it's not swearing. It's being friendly.

He looked back at her, considering the possibility of protest. He'd taken to being critical, lately. Monica thought he enjoyed testing her. Any minute now, he'd call her a liar just to see what she'd do. Cheating, she popped a mint in his mouth, a stopper. It worked. By the time she looked back, the teen-faced girl and child were on the other side of the road, on their way. Being judgemental about strangers was cheap but Monica found she was doing it anyway. It drove her crazy the way nearly everybody pushed the buggy with the kid eyes-front, so all he could see was the terrifying advance of cars and buses and blank-faced strangers, and everybody doing something made it *normal*. That Monica had pushed Calum's buggy the other way round so they could see each other instead had only made her a crank. *Nothing-the-Easy-Way Monica,* the health visitor called her in that squeaky-clean voice: *that boy's got you wrapped round his little finger!* Clearly, it still rankled. *Normal* had a lot to answer for. *Normal* often slipped past any duty to be kind. In the distance, she saw the little boy's rabbit tumble over the side of the buggy, an elderly man picking it up, holding it to the raised buggy hood with a smile. Calum's hand tugged again, drawing her attention back to rights.

Green man, he said. Look. She had barely registered the fact before he was way ahead, striding onto the crossing without a second glance. That everyone would obey the rules, that nothing bad would happen if he did too, he took for granted. His whole world rested on a terrifying level of trust that shocked and moved her in equal measure.

Wait for mum, she called, knowing he was already out of earshot. Wait for me.

A Wednesday at the tail end of summer meant there was plenty of room on the ferry. She'd been looking forward to it: last day of freedom, a final fling before first day of school. The uniform was already bought and paid for: blazer, tie and v-necked jumper, all slightly too large and grungy green; a first pair of proper shoes; a three-pack of shirts complete with cardboard inside the collars and far too many pins. Apart from the tie, which made him suspicious, he liked everything. Dreary colours and full-limb coverings meant growing up. At least for boys. She imagined folding his orange and lime green tee-shirts, nestling them away in a drawer as souvenirs. Today, however, they could wear what they liked, take the ferry to Millport for fun. Uncle Peter had taken Monica there when she was small, probably for the same reason. She couldn't remember much about it now, just sugar dummy-tits strung up like dead balloons outside an ancient sweetie shop that smelled of tobacco, a rack of benches on the beach. Nostalgia was the right mood, Millport the right place for runaways in cahoots. Monica pointed out the snail-line of family saloons creeping up the metal ramp, the gulls hovering over the stern, then fished his sunglasses out of her pocket and settled them on his nose.

You look great in those, she said. Like an explorer.

He looked over the top of the blue and red rims. Spiderman, he said. They're Spiderman specs. I'm Spiderman on his holidays.

She pressed his nose with the tip of her finger, said *Beep*.

Stop that, he said, as she knew he would. He swatted her like a fly. You behave.

Huge, clown-beaked gulls followed the boat for the whole short trip, skimming between water and sky. Monica had remembered to bring bread, so they took turns, like feeding ducks in the park. She held hers out, allowing the bolder birds to pluck the pieces from her fingers. Calum threw instead, crunching his eyes against the wind to see them catch in mid-air. His skin didn't crease, she thought. Whatever he did with his face, it unfolded again smooth as soap. When the bread was done, they played I-Spy, a game that bored Monica stiff but that Calum liked anyway. At least, he *had* liked it: these days, it would be more accurate to say he preferred it to nothing. They managed two games straight, then he started kicking over the game's unwritten traces. When his fourth shot, something beginning with W was not wind, not waves, but wombat, she packed it in. I-Spy's days were most likely numbered. After a trip to the engine room, the café and the slot machine, they came back on deck for a view of the near-nothing mainland: the steeple clock shrunk to an exclamation mark, the prim little holiday town of Largs turned to Trumpton. Monica almost said so, then caught herself. He was too big for little-boy tv references now. Instead, she pointed out a man in a hat holding an important-looking rope.

Is that the captain? he said, hauling his belly onto the ship's rail, feet dangling. Monica guessed it might be. Calum waved, tentative, but the man didn't see. They watched the island lurching closer, the people onshore waiting to return. Calum wriggled, his feet swinging.

Did dad phone? he asked suddenly.

No, Monica said. He might have sent a card, though.

Then again, he might not. The new girlfriend was pregnant, rotten with morning sickness. Or so she had heard. These days Calum's dad had a lot of new things on his mind: it was what *moving on* meant. Everything about life since Calum had been waiting to see. Just the two of them these days at least made life more settled. She had never thought one day she'd long for at least a little predictability, but here she was. It had its charms. The dad subject dropped and they watched the harbour instead, teetering closer. When it was time, the notional captain threw the rope. A man onshore caught the hawser, looped and hauled, and the boat thudded home on a buffer of tyres. It was neat; the sort of service some folk offered strangers that made Monica feel cherished; the business of safe hands.

Come on, Calum roared. He jumped down, flexed his fingers. Last one on the bus is a dumpling.

It'll be me then, Monica thought, mock-hurrying. I'm the dumpling. It's always me.

The back of the bus was the only place he'd sit these days, but at least the windows were clean. Single houses thickened into a row of bungalows, some with palm trees. The terminus was only feet from the sea. On the other side of the road, a chip shop, a pub and a pink shop strung with plastic buckets lined the road back. Calum chose the sea, scrambling down the nearest grass verge. Reaching the rocks, however, ground him to a stop. She looked, trying to see what it was that made him suddenly hesitant. The trails of algae, maybe, slimy to climb; barnacles and shale that looked sharp enough to cut. Abruptly, he turned and asked for a drink.

But we're just here, Monica said.

Don't care. I'm thirsty.

There was a hint of fretfulness in his voice, of backing off. She herded him across the road without protest, hoping they'd find the toilets soon. Inside the shop, he chose a purple drink. She looked at his white tee-shirt and shorts, but he caught her and promised to be careful. He promised twice.

Ok. She handed over the coins. But you're buying. On you go.

After a moment's indecision, he put the money on the counter top and pointed, embarrassed. It was not a confident performance, but at least he hadn't backed out. He got what he wanted. The rack of magazines at his back was awash with zombies and monsters, a green Samurai chopping someone's face in two with an axe. On the rung above, a woman with her legs apart showcased a little banner with the words MORE INSIDE in scarlet.

Here, she said, drawing Calum away so he wouldn't see. Put the straw in by yourself.

It was a good move. Putting the straw in was a fine art by now, one he took pride in. She stood back, giving him time. First, he scratched the plastic cover over the little hole with one nail, then carefully scrambled the straw out of its sheath on the back of the carton. It took both hands, but he didn't drop the box. He poked the straw in, knowing from experience to stand back, avoid the spit-back of juice that was likely to result. This time, it didn't. He smiled, lipped the straw into his mouth and sucked, then stretched his boxless arm at forty-five degrees, hand balled into a fist. Superman. Monica smiled. Since the joke was made, he set Superman aside and sat on the lip of the kerb, watching passing dogs till the drink was done, then scanned the horizon. It wasn't OCD: it was a perfectly natural desire to do the right thing. Litter went into a bin, so now they had to find one. If not, he'd carry the damn thing all day. Two streets away, still within sight of the sea, they found their best option attached to a lamp post – already full and spilling banana skins, but it served. Monica pressed the rubbish down with her hands, wincing: Calum reached up on his toes, spilling nothing at all. Finished, he smacked his hands and looked around, thrilled with his life.

Well, he said. What'll we do now?

Monica checked her watch. There would be no time for the crazy-golf if they didn't go now. She struck a racing pose, a challenge. They ran all the way. These days, everything was running.

The course was no different to the last time Monica had seen it as a girl. One look at the plain concrete assault courses told her ricochets would be likely, but they could always duck. Her stick – a *ladies' stick*, the hire man insisted – was too short and Calum cheated and nobody cared. What mattered was the daftness of the thing, hitting golf balls around windmills and through the tiny castle moat, Calum winning. They took the ball and putters back but the attendant was no longer there, just a man, holding a child by the hand.

Stop fucking whining, he said. You've had plenty, you greedy wee cunt.

The child said nothing. Three, Monica thought. Younger than Calum. Think I'm made of fucking money.

Monica glanced at Calum. Once, he'd kicked a woman at the train station for dragging a pup on a leash till it started choking, just lashed out. Before that, he had always been nervous of strangers. Now, he was changing. Some things upset him more than others. People breaking rules or being mean was a Big Deal. Being mean to animals was the biggest deal there was. Maybe it was her fault. He had seen her ordering teenage boys to cut out shoving the wee ones off the school bus at home time, telling girls effing and blinding in the street to behave. But seeing it in *him* was unsettling. She didn't want him reacting now. The boy was tiny, but the man was big. Broad shouldered. He narrowed his eyes at Monica, then yanked the boy aside to let her past.

Don't know they're born these days eh? he said. He raised the boy's wrist as he spoke, high enough to lift him momentarily off the ground. Do they?

No, Monica said. She looked at the boy, tried a smile. He looks like you.

It was true. Matching leather bomber jackets, jeans, frighteningly white tennis shoes; their hairstyles exactly the same. The man kept his eyes on her, saying nothing.

And I'm sure he's a great boy really, she said. I mean, I'm sure he's—

Aye. When he feels like it. The man snorted, dropped the boy's arm as though he'd lost interest in the whole thing, as though he might even be embarrassed, and started walking. The boy, after a second, ran after.

Monica put the clubs back on the counter. There was no one to take them, just an honesty box and a handwritten sign. LOST BALLS 50p. She found some loose change for the hell of it, let Calum slot it in the box coin by coin till it was gone.

Well, she said, drawing a deep breath. That man was in a bad mood. Her heart was thumping.

Pig, Calum said. A big, fat shit-pig.

Monica said nothing. Nothing at all.

Back at the bay, an ice-cream van had parked in the bus bay, Tom and Jerry looking near-antique painted on one side. Monica bought two cones with extra raspberry sauce and Calum ate all of his, no spills. A Jack Russell ate most of Monica's since it was offered then followed them all the way down the prom before realising there was no more.

Gone, Calum said. See? He opened his hands. The dog checked. It was true. All gone.

Sticky, they scrambled down the verge not far from where they had started. Monica found a rock pool and doused her hands. Calum held back.

There'll be beasts in there, he said. Crabs and things.

No there won't, she said. For goodness' sake, it's just water. Like in the sink at home. He stared at her. Ok, she sighed. It's not really. Let's be logical instead. She looked him in the eye, became a teacher. If there's crabs in this pool, they'd be babies, right?

He nodded, once.

And if they're babies, they'd run away the minute they saw your giant mitts coming in through the ceiling of their house. Right? It stands to reason. They're more scared of you – I know, he said. Than you are of them. I know.

Clearly, she'd used that line before. Monica gave her hands another dip, tried to look nonchalant. The water was freezing. After a moment, Calum dipped a single finger into the pool, pulled it back out fast.

It's cold, he said. But his resistance was already less. Monica dipped her hands again then slowly, without breaking the mood, stood and slicked her palms down the seams of her jeans, a show of how to get them dry. From the corner of an eye, she saw her son take it on, running his fingers awkwardly in the cold water, then dredging them over his shorts, not sure this was a sane thing to do at all. Behind him, the water was glittering, sharp; the sand a dark buff-gold. Strewn across it, as though it had been put there to spite anyone tempted to find the scene picture-pretty, was litter: tampon cases, polystyrene pizza shapes with most though not all of the pizza missing, empty wrappers and cups. Four cans, one wearing the plastic hoop they had once shared, sat near a clump of sea pinks, oozing.

It's a mess. Calum stood at her elbow. He pointed at a tumbled coffee tub, two whelks coiled inside.

Yep, she said. But one man's mess – she scooped the cup out of its puddle – is another man's treasure.

What's that mean? he said.

It means, she said, looking him in the eye, we can beach-comb. And this – she rattled the invaders back into the pool, showed him the cup was clean – is what we put our treasure in. Ok? Anything good we find on the sand goes in here and not my back pocket.

First hauls were cigarette packets, the gold lettering attracting him, she presumed. One had a cigarette still inside, dry as toast in its foil lining. Next, a piece of wet cardboard with a picture of a gun on it, the plastic moulding where the toy had been now empty.

At least it's the right shape, he said. That could be useful.

Sure, she said. The shape of a gun is always handy.

It's explorers, he said. Excitement was lifting him now, letting a younger, less self-conscious boy out for his last adventure. Like a desert island. He jumped on top of a rock. I'm the doctor explorer and you're – you're somebody else.

Monica smiled. Nurse, the assistant, the driver, the pupil to his teacher – she'd done those: now she attained the lofty status of *somebody else*. Maybe he was feeling it too – the encroachment of compulsory schooling, other people's rules. The beginning of separateness. This time tomorrow, he'd still be four years old, but he'd be in uniform, squaring up to alien expectations. She watched him running on the shale, all fear of falling forgotten. He had no idea, she thought, shivering as the breeze caught her neck, how vulnerable he was. Of course not. Already he had found something new, was waving for her to come and see. When she got there, he was pointing at a nest of split razor-shells, polythene bags, at something pallid. She picked it up, turned it in her hands. Bone. A tiny pelvis, almost; two empty sockets and a bowl the colour of clotted cream, dried weed clinging to its hollows.

It's a skull for horses, he whispered.

She looked at him, wondering where that had come from.

It is, he said. I've seen them before.

It's awful small for a horse, she whispered back.

He got down on his hunkers, looked her in the eye. That's because it's shrunk.

His face was professorial. Whether he was in character or not was hard to say, but she did not smile. Mere *somebody else*, she was in no position to argue.

Doctor, she said, nodding, if you say so, that's what it is.

She dropped it with the rest into the cup and he dusted down his hands. Doctors, he said, were *never* wrong.

The rest of the beach gave them four brown feathers, some orange pebbles, a handful of jointed clamshells, a doll's head, a cache of egg-cases, a claw and a baby sock that had been chewed by something with no staying power. Last, some glass pebbles, glycerine-clear till lifted from the water, when they turned a cloudy green. There were more in the pool, brown and white.

Are they treasure? he said. I mean, *real* treasure? Diamonds or something?

The word *maybe* was hovering on the tip of her tongue. She fought with it, then decided better.

No. It's glass, she said. People bring bottles, then the bottles get smashed, then over a long time, with the sand and the rocks and everything, the pieces of glass get worn

down. Smooth. Like this. She held one out in her palm.
See?

Calum picked it up, drew his finger along its side.

No blood, he said. Glass that doesn't cut. Their eyes
met. That's sort of magic, he said. So it's ok. Magic's worth
money.

Between magic and money: that was the stage he was
at. A whole new boy was coming up to meet her, someone
surprising. He laughed as he gathered the chunks of glass
together, his baby teeth near-transparent in the clear light.
Monica slipped the whole lot into her back pocket, aware
she'd said she wouldn't do anything of the sort.

Caught me, she said.

He grinned.

They turned at the natural conclusion of the sand. Out past
the range of offshore hills, rain was misting in from the
mainland. Calum ran ahead, then stopped sharply, poking
one slatted shoe out in front of him. Monica thought he was
trying to avoid the grit getting into his sandals to begin
with, the sand having turned again to shale. Closer, she saw
little round patties, like eggs left to dry in the sun, slumped
on the pitted shoreline. Calum's eyes were round.

Jellyfish, she said. Calum looked worried. They're animals, she said.

You can see through them, he said, horrified. Into their
guts.

It was true. Pebbles were clearly visible beneath the

sprawled, plasma-yellow bodies, tinted to match. Monica poked one with the tip of her sandal, dusting the gummy surface with sand.

It's still an animal, she said. They live in the water most of the time, floating. But if the tide turns too fast, they get stuck.

It's got no legs, he said.

No legs, no fins, she added. Just this.

He nodded, all trust, then scanned the beach. Feet away were more. The biggest had a rock in the middle and was bust to bits, its body turning cloudy. This close it looked liked a blood-clot under slow-frying albumen, an eye in need of surgery.

Is it sore? he said, slowly.

It's dying, Monica said. Maybe dead already. That's why it's going white.

Calum kept looking, horrified. Why is it dying? What happened?

This was a hard one.

Well – Monica took a deep breath – sometimes people aren't good. They attack things that can't fight back.

Why?

Maybe they don't think hard enough. She hoped he wouldn't get stuck on a *why?* groove. Answers for *why* were never easy.

But it can't run away, he said. They should take it back in the water. They should behave.

Yes, they should. But they don't. Maybe they hurt it – her

voice faltered – they hurt it *just because* it can't stop them. Because they can.

Calum's face grew dark. Monica told herself not to cry. She was too soft, her mother said. She'd pass that on if she wasn't careful, make her own son into bully-fodder. Actually, her mother had used a cruder word, a word that drove Monica crazy, but the advice itself was not so easy to dismiss. She fought it now, aware something this slight made her weak. These soft, transparent animals, open as wounds, lying where the tide settled them to simply wait. Stranded, they had no defences. Nothing. She could have wept.

Maybe, she said. Maybe they don't feel pain the way people do.

Her voice petered out. There was nothing else to say. They stood together a little longer, looking down. Then Calum made a move. With no telling what made the choice, he started running. That was new too. He charged at things these days, just ran. He ran all the time, refusing to hold her hand. She hoped she'd remember that tomorrow, not be selfish. *On the way to school, do not hold his hand. Do not cry and do not hold his hand.*

Suddenly, the ice-cream dog appeared from nowhere and ran beside him, thrilled to bits. Calum was sociable, not like her. He'd run till he was tired. Then he'd come back. There was no need to follow, no need to worry. He'd be back.

On the other side of the dunes, a couple of toddlers

were digging. Not far away, someone that might be their big sister was struggling towards them with a filled pail, spilling water that made moon-holes on the sand. She watched for a moment, then realised there was more to it. The sand itself; something about the texture of the sand on this particular stretch of beach. Mere inches away, the line of her footprints showed it too, the sides of their sole-shaped hollows refilling, crumbling in on themselves as she watched. The sand was moving. Like restless demerara, what had once been solid rock was not done yet. The whole beach was tilting itself down as she stood here, moving on. Sands. She smiled at the thought. They really did shift. A tiny crab fought its way from under a boulder, waving his legs. She'd show Calum when he came back.

She saw him then, her boy running back. Behind him, three older lads were kicking a plastic ball, squealing a commentary in unbroken voices.

Can I? Calum was shouting, his voice all but blown away by the wind. He arrived breathless, big-eyed. Can I play with them? He pointed. They've got a football. Kind of.

She looked across, undecided, trying to gauge something she couldn't put her finger on. They were boys. Just boys.

Oh all right then. Why not? I'll shout you when the bus comes.

Calum ran five steps, stopped and turned. Did you keep my pebbles?

For a moment, Monica couldn't think what he meant.

The pebbles, he said. The magic glass?

She rattled her back pocket, nodded.

Ok, he said. He thumbed up, and went back to his running.

One day, Monica thought, watching him go, she'd get a camcorder. For now, she hoped her memory lasted. She saw his white shirt billow as his hand lifted, waving. He did not look back. His eyes were on the boys ahead, their welcome. They shouted him on.

looking at you

There's glitter as they walk around behind there, black teeshirts making the bottles come and go. Through a burr of other people's talk, the soft clash of glasses, there's Nick at the end of the counter, slivering slices of citrus so thin you can see through them from here. Sheer. There's enough for twenty on the board and he's going for one more, the little yellow tit of the end of the lemon still cupped inside his palm. He lifts them like they're cards when he's done, a suit and a half in one hand, drops them into a water-jug, jumps back when the splash comes. It gets him anyway. He looks over at Marc hoping Marc's seen the drama and winks, swirling the water-jug like a brandy bowl, hips swaying like a stripper's. He pours himself a glass and drinks, his pinkie and fourth finger cocked. No tattoos, no rings, no friendship bracelets; dear god no watch. His arms are completely naked. Rod comes, a tray of half-pints in both fists. He slides behind Nick to half-way then stops, shifting the tray to the one hand like a barbell, whisper-ing. His double earring rubs against itself when he tilts

his head, whispering secret barman stuff, almost kissing
Nick's neck. Rod's lips are a toddler's lips, soft and fat and
sheeny. He and Nick have the same short hairstyle, necks
like mushroom stalks, translucent under the bar lights.
They don't need to exchange looks, just smile looking in
the same direction, crotch to arse as Nick goes on slicing,
listening, his nape bared. Rod flips the tray higher when
Marc comes over too; it's right up on the balls of his fingertips. Now there's room for three. Whatever it is he says they
all laugh and you've never seen so many perfect teeth. All
those creamy ivories. The open mouths attract Steven, ten
tan fingers dripping from the glasses he's just washed so
he has to hold them up like a flamenco dancer to save the
others from splashes. Little rivulets of water snake down
his arms, veins coursing on the surface. Nick looks thin as
a stick beside him, all angles and pipecleaner bends and
fuzzy to the touch you bet you bet. Steve is square and
olive-skinned, early Elvis sideburns with a fine silver chain
tipping his breastbone. A stiff chest, a heartbeat you'd be
able to hear out loud, feel if he stood close. He's the most
beautiful man you ever saw and he only has eyes for Marc.
Marc knows and doesn't mind. Not at all. Marc's straight
as a cucumber, so white he's blue. Celtic. Opening his shirt
would make you snow-blind. Temporarily. His nipples
would be like bites. He has red, red cockscomb hair. And
he's not looking at the barmaid. Nobody's looking at the
barmaid. He's looking at you.

and drugs and rock and roll

Lucille was singing *Dream a Little Dream of Me* with the late Mama Cass and none of the notes were right. None of Cass's were right either but it wasn't her fault. It was the batteries. Lucille's boyfriend brought her in a bag of ancient tapes that she played all day, round and round till the music melted like something out of a horror movie. It wasn't there yet but it was coming: it always did. Mary-Lou, who hardly ever spoke, piped up to say she hoped Lucille's crappy machine would blow up and take Lucille's fucking face off when it did, then went back to her rap music as if rap was spelled with a w and meant comfort. It was not a comfort, not in Alma's opinion: it was a misogynist's wet-dream. Mary-Lou lip-synched the word *bitch* so many times a day she had stopped noticing she was doing it and it drove Alma crazy. This was what happened: you thought you had problems till you found a whole new set in whatever ward they put you in. At least Dianne wasn't crying because Dianne wasn't in, and Roxanne's baby-voiced Boy Band, along with Roxanne, was absent. Further down the corridor, some lousy American movie was shooting the living daylights out of the day room tv and Victor was on the warpath.

The thing with Victor wasn't new. He'd been jumpy since tea-time, hanging around when the plates were being cleared, tutting at cutlery as though his personal disapproval would make it behave. Now, in those low-slung jeans he liked and zooming in like a heat-seeking missile on Roxanne's bed, he was ready to give us a go at the same. Alma watched him touching Roxanne's stuff – magazines, the cards she ranged on top of her locker – as though they might hold clues. The elastic band of his man pants said GUESS.

Nothing good on the telly?

Victor, still with his back to Alma, was letting her know he felt watched. He opened Roxanne's biggest card, the one with a duck and the words CHEER UP! in pink glitter, and scrutinised its insides.

There's never anything good on, she said.

I know, Victor said, his voice flat. I was being *ironic*. He put the duck card down, picked up a teddy bear in a nurse's cap and looked under its vest. I was making light of the fact I know that if you're looking at my underwear you must be bored stiff. Which is to say I was making a joke.

He put the bear aside and stuffed his hands under Roxanne's pillows instead. A joke to pass the weary hours haha. Turn that racket down, Lucille, eh?

Lucille paid no attention. Victor sighed and started ferreting behind the headboard, trying not to be annoyed.

And Alma remembered she hadn't seen Roxanne at tea-time either. Terry sat next to her, ate his meal in silence, then stood up to drink his milk in one go and wipe his mouth with the back of his hand. He did this routine every time. But even Terry, who minded nobody's business but his own, had noticed something not right. *Your pal's no here.* It was true. Roxanne did not eat much, but she was usually *there.* Thinking about it now, Alma realised she hadn't seen Roxanne all day.

Victor, is Roxie ok?

Victor patted down the mattress, both hands; didn't answer. Victor? I'm asking. Has she had another fit?

Not your business. Victor peeled the slips off the pillows, dropped them on the floor, and stared down at them.

I'm just asking, Alma said. Look, maybe if you tell me what you're looking for I can help.

Victor, stripping the under-sheet, the plastic protector, the second under-sheet didn't even blink. I'm just doing my job, he said.

I know. But she's not got anything. Not this time. There's no stash.

Victor ignored her.

If she was going to pinch pills she wouldn't hide them in her bed, would she? She knows it would be the first place you'd look. She's not daft, Victor.

Alma, he said. He raised an eyebrow. Enough.

She shrugged, went back to looking at the floor, the sweetie wrappers and spine-cracked magazine under Roxanne's bed.

PARTY FOR SYRIA'S WAR ORPHANS.
JORDAN'S BABY HEARTBREAK.

Mary-Lou started bitching again, her bed creaking as she rocked.

Somebody ought to do something about that lassie, Victor said. He opened Roxanne's locker drawers, forking his fingers through her letters, her unwashed tights. Pardon my French, but she's fucking obscene.

Alma put her head round the door of the half-way kitchen just in case but it was only Dianne. Dianne couldn't leave the kettle alone.

Tea? She held out a striped mug, not waiting for an answer. It's spare, she said. I like two on the go. Doctor says I've got tannin on the brain.

Alma took the mug, clocked the lipstick mark on the rim. Thanks, she said, settling the cup to one side. Thanks.

Victor's in a bad mood eh? Dianne held her tea on her lower lip, tipping back steady mouthfuls. I've just been up the 4M and they said the same. Somebody said Victor left some old guy in a puddle of shit for an hour before he could be bothered shifting him. At least, so he said. Lazy pig.

We all have bad days, Alma said.

He's not supposed to have bad days, Dianne snorted. He's supposed to look after people. That's the whole idea behind nursing, you know? *Care*. I asked him last week to get me stuff for my dentures so they'd sit right and he never bothered. He's lazy.

Alma said nothing. It was too late at night for this kind of thing. Moaning. Things undone. All it did was make getting to sleep harder. She kept her eyes on the mug, trying not to smell the contents. Like mulch. Like some kind of decay.

Tell you something else, Dianne said. He shopped Roxanne for pinching towels. I know it's annoying but godsake. *Everybody* pinches towels.

Did Declan manage in? Alma was fishing for another subject and knew it. Moaning about Victor was too easy.

No. Dianne looked up. No the night. He'd be here all the time only our Sandra's chair is *verboten* on the bus. We've no car, no lift we could get or nothing. And Sandra's not able to stay in on her own, so that's that.

Alma knew next to nothing about Dianne's daughter except for the wheelchair. Why she used it was not discussed. It was nobody's business. In Psychiatric, illness in general was nobody's business. Asking too much was *not done*. It was *poking one's nose*. Sometimes, Dianne's husband came in during his lunch break if he was on the right shift and sat at Dianne's bedside till he was due back at the mortuary. Once, he'd been a night porter, now he only did days. He didn't speak much when he came in, just sat, holding his wife's hand. He had big, powerful hands. A Gentle Giant.

Your bloke was a no-show as well, Dianne said. What's his name. He didny come.

Gerry, said Alma. His name's Gerry. No, he didn't.

Or your mum. Sad for her, eh? Mothers take it hard if there's anything wrong with their wee ones, no matter how big the wee ones get. Sandra's near twenty-five but in my head, she's ten. She'll always be ten.

Look, Alma said. I need to go now. Sorry. I was just looking for somebody and looked in. I really need to go. Dianne's eyes lifted from the still-fullness of Alma's cup, disappointed. Was it no good? I can make you another one.

No, I'm just looking for somebody, Alma said. I'm off. Thanks anyway.

It's no bother, Dianne said, getting to her feet. I'll make you a fresh one. You can get it when you come back.

Alma backed to the kitchen door, called her goodbyes over one shoulder, walked. Half-way down the corridor, she realised the mug was still in her hand. Lukewarm, the teabag still inside. She slid sideways into the nurse's toilet and poured the lot into the bowl. Auburn water in the toilet bowl, wood-tint red. Dianne's insides must be that colour, she thought, flushing, watching the tea caught up in the vortex from the cistern. Even at short acquaintance, they'd know when they looked. Dianne's tea always left a mahogany wash behind.

Roxanne was nowhere obvious, nowhere else. The round-up would start soon, names, notes, night allocation, bed: the trolleys were banging around already. Wherever Roxanne was, she'd be roped in with the rest and tucked up in less than an hour whether she wanted it or not. Maybe looking for her was bogus: just a reason to escape the ward. Nights were difficult. At the best of times, Alma found nights and giving in to sleep difficult. Roxanne had most probably been an excuse to work off a little nervous energy. After Dianne, Lucille and Victor, Alma realised she had been looking for someone that wasn't them, but the someone wasn't necessarily Roxanne. Who she wanted to see, it struck her now, was Michelle.

The first time Alma saw Michelle was three weeks ago, doing Mrs Kidd's hair behind a glass ward partition: a thin, blond thing with the most notorious screamer in Psychogeriatric sitting silent beneath her hands as she curled and pinned. She was too young for new staff, too slight. The girl, whoever she was, looked up. Alma expected a V sign. Instead, the girl raised one hand and shifted it, stiffly, side to side. A greeting. Alma, without thinking, waved back.

Admitted only a week before, fifteen, the owner of a working hair dryer, Michelle was *new*. She liked sitting in with the older women, she said; older women told better stories. That she was allowed to join them she took as a compliment, but she was never unsupervised – not just in Psychogeriatric but all the time. Michelle had a minder. Serious suicide risks, anorectics, unpredictable mood-swingers were all candidates, but not many actually got one. Michelle's parents were pushy. Michelle got one. She got Geraldine. In the bath, the toilet, next to her at the refectory table, checking on her in bed till she fell asleep, Geraldine's job was just to be there. In case. Which meant there was possibly something more going on with Michelle and the rotating blades inside the hairdryer than showed on the surface, but nobody said so out loud. Asking outright went beyond an unstated pale. There was little enough privacy in here: people had a right if they chose to stay buttoned. Michelle, though: Michelle was a whole different level of plausible. It made Alma uncomfortable at first, the apparent self-possession, the angel face. Maybe she was afraid whatever it was Michelle suffered from would come out when she least expected it and be too terrible to bear. But Michelle acted more ok than most of the staff. She did not complain or behave unreasonably; her mascara did not run or her lipstick miss its target. She did not ask for things all the time. She did not harp and she did not yearn. Which was why, when Michelle picked up the book on Alma's locker and lingered with it, opening the cover out wide to see the whole picture and run her finger over the author's face, it had made an impression.

Trocchi, she had said. She ran her finger down the spine. My boyfriend says he's cool.

Mine too, Alma said. Not my kind of cool, but there we are. Michelle smiled.

Gerry that gave it to me. Boyfriend. Said he thought I might *learn something*.

Did you? Michelle flipped the book over, scanned the back. Did you learn something?

Hard to say. Gerry didn't specify what the thing I might

learn was supposed to be and if I hit the target, I still missed it. It's about this guy taking drugs and not fitting in and thinking he's as cool as shit. Well, Gerry's idea of *as cool as shit* anyway.

Michelle laughed.

Poster boy for the revolution kind of thing. I thought he was a bit – well – up himself. Don't let me put you off, though. You might *love* it.

Michelle laughed again, bell-bright. And, noticing it, Alma laughed too. Meaning it. It felt like laughing again for the first time after you'd forgotten how. Lying in bed that night with the lights out, Mary-Lou *bitching* away in the next but one bed, it made her feel almost warm. It made her want to give Michelle something back. Nothing big, just a *thanks*. And what she had to hand was the book. Who knew? Michelle might think it was the bee's knees. Even if she didn't, though, it was the giving part that mattered. Between home visits and OT sessions and one thing and another it had slipped, the way so many things did, into the stuckness that brewed in every corner of the unit. Whether it was the medicine, the place itself, the act of surrender it had taken to come in in the first place didn't matter: it was there all right, and difficult to shake. Which meant *do it now*. As she waited in the corridor dreading the medicine trolley and the twilight zone, fearful the idea of doing something out of wanting to would be lost altogether, Alma grasped something important. Wanting to meant doing it *now*.

Inspired, she walked the length of the corridor. There was no sign of Michelle. A ward, the day room, Psychogeriatric and the kitchen the same. The library that had no books or seats in it and the nursing bay showed open doors but no one inside and the queue at the hot drinks machine was all older women, the tea and coffee generation. Young things more often zeroed in on the soft drinks machine for an allocation of tooth-rot with their refreshment. No Geraldine either. Maybe they were huddled in the ward toilets, Geraldine checking Michelle didn't have a razor blade concealed in her socks or whatever it was Geraldine did. Unless she was hiding in the lift, there was only one public place left to try. The Quiet Room.

The Quiet Room was quiet partly because it had a piece of foolscap with SHHHHHH written on it single-tacked to the wall, but more because hardly anybody went in there because it had all the charm of a box room. It was also freezing. One table, three chairs, a broken heater – nothing else. Staff sometimes put flowers there to keep them fresh and OT went now and then to do those origami sessions or whatever the hell it was they did that needed a table, but that was it. Alma found it the day she was admitted and it suited her purposes: a place she could jam the door with a chair and cry all day if she felt like it was exactly what she was after. Nobody came. After that, she sneaked into the Quiet Room a lot, met the odd nurse hunting for a vase, but no one else. She could imagine Michelle being curious, trying the room out for size. If she had given Geraldine the slip, it would be a place to hide.

Alma headed down the ante-room corridor and found the door. It had been painted recently, still smelled faintly of linseed. There were no bars of light around the frame to suggest occupation, nothing to hear. Alma stood back and turned the handle.

The first thing was the cold. Someone had opened the window, as wide as the chain allowed. All that showed in the gap was the dark above the chemical plant milky with light pollution; beyond that, thick black. No stars, just black. The second thing was that someone else was in here too. Someone in the far corner of the room sitting on one of the bucket chairs. Not Michelle. The air was too heavy. Too disturbed. You didn't have to be able to see to know who that was. It was Roxanne.

Hello, Roxanne said.

Hi. Alma kept her voice low, kept it calm. Roxanne had bad nights.

I'm just sitting, Roxanne said. Don't put the light on. It hurts my eyes.

Roxanne's hair, eye sockets like inkwells, the curtain shifting. In daylight, the curtain was sun bleached, patterned with stains like water damage. The carpet worn, easy to trip on the threadbare bits if you weren't careful. Standing on it now felt like standing on sand. There was nothing to hear but Roxanne's asthmatic breathing.

Looking for peace? she said.

No, Alma said. Looking for Michelle.

The one that looks like a wee lassie? The one that's cutting herself?

Alma said nothing.

She is, though. They've got somebody watching her. As if it'll make any difference.

You've not seen her? Alma said.

She wouldny come here, Roxanne said. Too quiet.

Michelle's quiet, Alma said.

Different sort of quiet. Roxanne drew on a fag in the dark, made the tip brighten her mouth, fade. She needs other folk to be there – she's the type that gets creeped out on her own. In here – look at it. There would be just her, by herself, no panic buttons. Well, just her if she got rid of that big sumph that hangs about her like a blanket.

Alma heard a sound like laughing, a cough.

She'd make anybody want to do themselves in, bloody Geraldine. You wonder they havny thought that through.

Alma felt now might be a good time to get away, but Roxanne hadn't finished.

Anyway, she's no here. Her folks will be lining her up for a transfer somewhere private. Bet you. They were in talking to the ward sister the other day. Their wee girl won't be around a place like this much longer.

A place like what?

Are you kidding? A holding pen – correction – an understaffed holding pen with sedatives that must drive the folk who work here crazy as well. It's not exactly The Priory, is it?

She laughed again and Alma could smell what she had been drinking. Something far too sweet. Fortified.

You, though. You're a different kettle of fish. I'd put money on it. You'll get beyond this place.

What does that mean? Alma heard a note of anger in her voice, knew to be careful.

It means, Roxanne said, there are different kinds of people end up in these places. There's people who don't get better and keep coming back because they can't see how not to, and there's people who push themselves to get out and stay out because they're smart. Nobody's fool. You? You're the second kind. Not right now mibby, not necessarily for always. But you'll get out and stay out. I can see it.

Alma said nothing.

One is a mistake, Roxanne said. Not a habit.

One what? Alma whispered.

Roxanne looked at her. Slower this time, Alma asked the same question again.

One *what*?

Roxanne sighed and slumped in her chair. Och, Alma. Don't pretend you don't know what I mean. She sounded on the verge of exasperation. Like Alma's mother. I read it on that thing in the office. It was lying on the desk and the ward sister goes out and just *leaves* it there and I read it. Secrets are no use in here. *So I read it.* Self-harm, depression, post-abortion syndrome *blah blah* – it's all there. If you don't want to talk about it that's fine, but I know why you're here.

You're not *special*. You tried DIY and they had to take you in to sort out the mess and now you're here. Right?

It's nothing to do with you, Alma said. At least, she wanted to. There were words the size of billboards in her head and nothing coming out of her mouth.

Right? Roxanne sighed.

Alma said nothing.

Your boyfriend no want it? Roxanne's voice was gentle. Or was it no like that? Did you not even tell him?

Alma said nothing.

Look, whatever. I'm not judging. I'm just saying you'll get yourself back together. Even if it was terrible, it's done. You're smart. You can work that out. Roxanne breathed out so hard Alma could taste sherry in her own mouth. One mistake is one mistake. Not like me.

Alma looked at Roxanne, the black shapes of her eyes in the dark.

I've had seven. *Seven*.

In the stillness, something dropped on the carpet, clunked dully onto the threadbare pile. A glass, tipped and bleeding a shadow out under Roxanne's sole, was just about visible when Alma looked down.

I *tried*. Pills, injections, pessaries – different stuff. Just kept happening. Some women get pregnant no matter what, I said. They thought I just liked being in the hospital.

For a moment, Alma thought Roxanne would cry. But Roxanne never cried. She didn't smile much and when she laughed it was seldom cheerful, but she never cried. That much was constant.

And I end up in here. Too young for a hysterectomy. I have *no underlying conditions.* Not medical reasons anyway. They think I might change my mind and there would be no going back *blah blah.* I mean, I get it. So here I am. Talking to Alma in the dark.

What age are you, Roxanne?

Twenty-five. Her features still indistinct, Roxanne inched closer. What age are you?

Alma said nothing for a long time.

It's not your fault, Roxanne said. What you did was just the one.

Leaning too close now, she began slipping from the edge of the chair altogether and Alma reached to catch her, settle her upright. It was important, somehow, that Roxanne should not fall.

You ok? Alma foraged with her shoe on the carpet, remembering the spilled glass, checking for shards. Are you cut?

No. I'm drunk.

As a skunk, Alma said. You're breaking all the rules.

Roxanne coughed and breathed in deep. I am, she said. And you're a cheeky cow.

I know, Alma said, Victor tells me that all the time. I am a cheeky cow.

Roxanne made her dry laugh again, lurched upright in stages. So far as Alma could see, she was intact.

Look, you better get back through to your ward, she said. I'll fetch a nurse eh? Roxanne snorted.

How did you get a glass in here? A bottle? They'll catch you if you keep doing it. You know they will. They'll get into trouble if they ignore it.

That's the difference between you and me, Roxanne said, sliding back into the seat, four-square. I don't fucking care. Breaking the rules is what I do.

I'll get Dianne, Alma said. Just sit tight. Don't go anywhere. I'll get someone, ok?

Ok, Roxanne said. Ok.

As she left, Alma heard Roxanne, a stage-whisper behind her back.

That Michelle, see when you find her? Tell her we're all in this world to help one another. She needs to stop being perfect. She needs to let somebody help her.

Alma walked faster. Twenty-five. Jesus. It both was and was not possible. Twenty-five.

Dianne was watching telly in the dayroom. Efficiency savings were not the same as cuts, someone was saying, big face all smiles on the screen. You have to understand that. The NHS will always be safe in our hands. It's a matter of priorities. Alma asked Dianne to get Roxanne out of the Quiet Room, not let the nurses find out she'd been drinking. Dianne was good at that kind of thing. She'd been a nurse once, long time ago. She could lift people, do rock-solid hospital corners. Dianne didn't ask any questions, she just covered tracks. After she left, Alma turned down the sound on the tv, leaving Terry staring at the blank square. He watched as a sedative: movement on the screen reassured him the world was turning properly. He saluted; whether to the tv or Alma was hard to tell. He hadn't been in the forces. She had already asked. He just liked to salute.

On the way out, she looked in at the Quiet Room door, heard nothing. Then went back down the corridor like nothing had happened. Past the laundry store, the towels with SOUTH CROSS GENERAL machine-stitched on every edge, past the dayroom and the dining room. Still looking: still no Michelle. The night-nurse, still working from a roster because she was new, asked her name.

Alma? she said. That's an old-fashioned name that. Your dad give it to you?

Grandad, Alma said. He liked a singer called Alma Cogan.

She was hot stuff, the nurse said. Alma Cogan for crying out loud. 1948. Older than me. Here.

She handed over a paper cup. Not diothepin, not protriptyline, not lorazepam or tranylcypromine either. Alma couldn't remember what the new stuff they had put her on was called but it made her less hazy. That meant it was working, she supposed. She knocked it back in one, handed back the cup.

She killed herself, did she not? Alma Cogan?

You could be right, Alma said. I hear some people do.

Tell me about it, the nurse said. She rolled her eyes.

Anyway, at least you're safe in here. Worse things happen at sea, love. Worse things happen at sea.

Lights out wasn't really.

Even if the overhead bulbs went off, light filtered in from the corridor, the nursing bay, the lifts. The reliable thing was medication. Alma's had been changed so many times she had lost track. Lying shivering under the hospital-issue blanket – bed was always cold till you surrendered to being there – Alma tried to work out if she had done anything today. Anything at all. Michelle was still missing. The book remained unloved, ungifted. Roxanne's bed was still empty. Over in Male, she could hear Terry singing *Rule Britannia*, big boomy voice full of wrong turns. When that stopped, the sound of Lucille creasing and uncreasing the polythene bag she kept in her locker for emergencies became more apparent. Dianne, who knew what that meant, got up and took Lucille's tape machine away and offered it up to the nursing bay to confiscate. It wasn't allowed at night: they usually forgot.

Forget it, Dianne shouted as Lucille started to cry. Not tonight. There's more than you in this ward, lady, and you're not playing this bloody thing tonight.

By the time she was back, Lucille had taken to whining. Whining was something Lucille could keep up for hours if she felt particularly bereft but tonight, it faded fast. Inexplicably, it was the silence that started Alma shaking. The hardest thing to keep in, especially in the dark, was

being the only one left awake. What got you then was yourself. No one else to blame. Only yourself.

Alma turned, crunched her eyes, determined not to cry.
Whatever had been lost today, she might find Michelle
tomorrow. How fast could somebody leave this place?
Gerry might visit if he had stopped being angry at her
being in here at all. *You don't belong in this place. You're volun-
tary. Come home, Alma. I've got stuff.* Stuff. Gerry believed in
stuff. Stuff was a fix and it worked every time. *Stuff* was not
prescription meds for sad bastards, it was edgy and cool as
shit and kissed with stardust. But it wasn't. Alma had had
no idea a high could drop you over the edge of a cliff and
leave you at the bottom when it was over. And even that
was not as bad as what followed the abortion, something
she occasionally still called *losing the baby* to avoid the good
Catholic prickle of the a-word itself. *Foetus*, Roxanne had
said, *Christ it was thirteen weeks. Stop blaming yourself.*

But she wasn't blaming herself. The depression just hit.
Some women, even when they didn't blame themselves,
just fell apart when the hormones shook back down. Like
baby blues. A reaction unattached to reason. The luck of
the draw.

Gerry didn't buy that. Psychiatric wards were for losers
and dregs and depression didn't exist: it was just learned
helplessness. He didn't believe in waiting or coming to
terms: this was the belief of an oppressor that would only
benefit if she gave in. Gerry believed in junk. The thing
was, he needed her to believe it too. Not wanting a baby

was a joint decision, he said. It was the two of them on the same path. But this, he said, this. This was politics. He had tears in his eyes. Didn't she realise being in this place was a terrible mistake? They'd break her and make her *ordinary*. He wouldn't watch it happen.

The thing was, she didn't believe what Gerry believed. No matter how hard he wanted her to. That in here, even with all the time-wasting and barely-getting-by and boredom that drove you to the bottom of where you had to go, she had grasped that the only thing that fixed anything at all was *coming to terms*. You had to look at what you were doing, at who you were. And if medicine helped her get her head back and didn't just blow it away, that was what she'd choose. This horrible, daily business of owning your own life. Answering to it. Knowing who you were.

She was moaning now, low and quiet, not much able to stop. It happened sometimes, a kind of screaming without sound that she recognised and was not afraid of any more. It was pain, that was all. In the long run, crying in the dead of night while the nurses clattered about outside and traded jokes was what being here was for. It let the pain in.

Water ran from her eyes and into her hair, wove cold little trails inside her ears. Embarrassing. Necessary, but embarrassing. Alma pushed up, blew her nose hoping it didn't bleed and swallowed what was left of pointless pride. She needed help and there was only one person around to fetch it.

Shivering, she slipped her feet to the floor and stumbled

into the corridor. Nobody bothered with her the first time. She had to ask twice, stand her ground, wait. Ask a third time, wait. But somebody did come. Somebody who said It's not as noisy as you think it is but prescribed something anyway and beetled back to her doctor place without speaking her name. Someone was bringing medicine: that was what mattered.

Finally, emerging through the haze of another ward's reflected light, there was Victor. His beard giving him away, his dark, dark eyes. Gazing upon the face of Victor as if he might be the risen Christ, Alma knew she had never been so pleased to see anyone in her life.

You being a nuisance? he said. Chirpy.

Yes, said Alma. A big nuisance.

The light from the corridor was enough, but Victor flicked on her bedside light, turned the glare to the wall so it didn't fill the whole ward. Courtesy. Alma held a tissue over her nose and watched him pick up her bedside book. Gerry's, then hers, now soon to be Michelle's book.

What's this, Alma? You reading again? They make you go daft, books.

He put the cup he carried down, held the book up instead, squinting like he couldn't see properly.

Trocchi. That how you say that name? Trocchi. Italian, eh?

I don't know, Alma said. It's not my book, just a loan.

All books are on loan, Victor said. A mock scowl. That's what my English teacher used to say. All books are on loan – they are made to pass on. Then she didn't like it if people stole them out the school library. Anyway, this Trocchi guy. I think I've heard of him.

Alma's eyes met Victor's, held for a moment before he looked back to the book blurb.

He wrote a book about heroin and stuff, expanded his mind on drugs so much it just kind of blew up. Ended up paranoid and skint. That's authors for you.

Alma almost smiled.

He's as cool as shit now, this guy. *Subversive*, it says here. Put his wife on the game or something to get the money for his habit and she died of hepatitis. *Radical subversive*. Cool as shit. Victor tipped the pills inside the cup to one side, counted them, put it back down and met her eyes. You're not looking too impressed with my summation, young lady.

No, Alma said. I'm not.

You not reckon he's up to much?

Alma looked at Victor, let her eyes fill because they would anyway, and turned away hoping he might not see. I'm just thinking, she said. I mean, putting his wife on the game to buy junk. She shook her head, eyes stinging. It has to be the least radical trick in the book, putting your wife on the game.

He's a hypocrite.

Well, now you point it out, Victor said, it's a shit way to behave. Selfish bastard. But it's done. They're dead, Alma. Let it go. Lie down. Try to sleep eh?

But it's not fair, she said. You think *Mr Subversive*, even for a moment, thought through the possibility of his going on the game instead?

You mean – Victor blinked – like being a rent boy or something?

Why not? I mean it. Why not take one for the team since the team was his own self, not let her carry the fucking can as if it was the natural choice. What a deadbeat. What an *arse*.

Oy, Victor said. Language. There's vulnerable women in here.

Alma breathed deep, tried hard to care about nothing. It had been a long time since she had been angry. She had almost forgotten how much it burned. Sorry, she said. Not your fault.

Not personally, Victor agreed. I'm one of the good guys. Right. Deep breath.

Alma took his advice, tried hard. She drew breath in till it hurt, let it shiver away too fast, not helping. Till it did. Five breaths, and it got slower. Her eyes stopped leaking.

There. Victor looked pleased. See? It works.

Bastard, though, eh? Barely a whisper. That Trocchi guy.

Victor pulled up the top sheet, shook his head. That's a terrible attitude you've got there, young lady. And a very dirty mind.

He was smiling all the same. So, after a fashion, was Alma. He leaned closer, lifted the cup to do what he had come to do.

What am I getting? she said.

Temazepam. Folk are paying over the odds for this in Paisley and here's you getting it free. Ready?

Alma nodded, shut her eyes.

Ok, here we go. He held the back of her head, tipped the cup into her mouth, then handed her the water. Alma swallowed twice and opened her eyes. Victor was still watching. He looked pleased.

Good girl, he said, crushing the cup in one hand, putting it into the bedside bin. When was the last time you heard that eh? *Good girl.*

He straightened the photos on the locker top, turned back for the last time.

Ok?

Ok, she said.

All right for some, he said. I'll be up all night. There's a new admit high as a kite on steroids through there, and I've a set of transfer papers to fill in. Michelle's folks are putting her somewhere else. The new lassie. She's on watch the whole time and still cutting. They think it's *our* fault. He shrugged. Here's less wages and less funding – same story every year. Ye canny win. It'll be private this time next year, you wait and see. You might be the last of a dying breed, Alma.

Alma wasn't sure if he was serious or just sad and sarcastic. Maybe he didn't know himself. He wasn't looking for affirmation anyhow, he was just talking. Which was better than him being in the huff. Maybe his shift was nearly up.

Oh – she left an address for you, by the way. Michelle in

Wonderland. I'll see you get it tomorrow – *if* you eat your breakfast. Ok?

Alma nodded.

Right. Don't worry about us taxpayers. You have a nice rest.

He handed back Lucille's tape machine on the way out, made her promise not to play it. Even before the squeak of Victor's shoes died away, Lucille was pressing buttons. It didn't matter. Alma told herself it didn't matter. It didn't matter because there was nothing she could do and anyway, something was working. Maybe not the pills, but her shoulders were trying to sink, her jaw to release. It might even be sleep.

Turning the pillow, she caught the outline of Terry in the corridor outside; Terry the Milk walking heavily in his striped pjs and carrying a teacup. He hesitated at the ward door, knocked back this drink, licked his white after-moustache. *The milk*, she heard him say. *The milk takes the heat from the meal.* Alma, still prone, saluted. Whether he saw her or not, Terry chose that moment to look up. He stared at the tiles coming off the ceiling, the broken night light; saluted both of them and walked on. As he faded from view, Alma's eyes were closing.

Soon, when the drugs kicked in, there would be quiet. Darkness.

She could wait a little longer, stick it out.

Soon, one way or another, she'd feel nothing at all.

that was then, this is now (1)

Sandra is not in the bath. Her parents are not in to nose her out in any case, but their idea of her is like she's fourteen or something, not the sophisticate she is now. She no longer spends so much time with nail varnish and cheap hair dye, both applied in streaks. She's not in the living room dancing alone and not in the kitchen, rooting for chocolate. All the lights are off downstairs. Even so, there's the sound of her, low and soft, on the musk-scented air: repeating the same, as yet indecipherable word with occasional intakes of breath. Is she singing? Doing exercises? Up there in the bedroom? At the top of the stairs are shoes on the carpet: four shoes, only two with high heels, three striped socks. A single earring, one of the ear-cuffs she wanted for Christmas, and the Furry Polar Bear she won at an indoor fun fair a million years ago when her friends were all girls and Furry Polar Bears were the *best thing ever,* lie any old how at the open door. Polar Bears are still something, but not what they were. You move on. You learn. You find *other things.*

Light from the street outside edges everything inside the noise-room blue: blue face-cream, an opened, blue lipstick on the top of the chest of drawers, an unopened blue packet fallen from the bedside table top are clear enough in outline. There is a hint of hemp. The gassy scent of perfume and smoke turned sweaty fills out; the air in this room could be wrung out for moisture if you tried. The light sticking and unsticking sound, not unlike Sellotape but softer, becomes more insistent. And a sucking sound. Two sucking sounds. There are people in here. Sandra – it must be Sandra – has her mouth full of someone, salt and hair between her teeth. You can hear her twist against the sheets.

Keep it in, she says, voice hissing like a freshly snapped can; *please Liam, please.*

Liam, whoever he is, makes a noise like a horse, like a tree falling slowly, a kind of whinnying groan then Sandra's voice like you never heard it before squeaking *Stay right where you are.*

Outlines in the low light make recognisable patterns: her back arched against the mattress, arms clasped beneath his shoulder-blades, her head lifting from the pillow. *Liam keep jesus keep it there please keep it in Liam jesus jesus please inside me now, now, now.*

Shhh, he says. Man's voice, low in the throat. *Jesus, Sandra, not yet not yet* – but he shudders suddenly, rattling the whole bed frame and everything in the room is taut. You can almost hear the clamming of her musculature, Sandra tightening everything she's got, her whole body fostering the last of his movement inside her so she comes too, big generous gurgles in her throat like she loves it, loves it, like she can't ever get enough. Can't ever. Get. Enough.

Enough.

After all that energy, all that release, just the sound of skin.

Unpeeling. Twin breaths decelerate for ages.

Then Sandra speaks, almost normal, almost in a voice her mother would recognise and know as her daughter. Almost.

Liam, she whispers. Li—am.

He says nothing but the air goes quieter. That guy must be lying very still indeed.

Can I say it?

What, he moans.

Again, she says. There is a long pause. I want it, she says, all over again.

And Liam, whoever he is, smiles so wide and generous you can *hear* it; the pleasure his mouth finds inside it just from listening to her is loosening the air. The springs creak as he turns towards her, the smile still in place.

You'll get cystitis if you keep this up.

Yes, she says. I don't care.

You'll get a rash, an infection from overuse, you greedy minx.

Yes please, she says. Give it your best shot.

Look, he says, more serious. Behave. You'll get pregnant if you do that thing you just did again.

Nah, she says. I'm not that kind. I'll wash myself out with vinegar.

And he laughs out loud, lets her catch him round the waist. Ready, despite herself, to wait till he's ready. Till she's propped herself up and drained. Till it starts all over. Again. No catching her out. Again.

Eric Blair, also known as George Orwell, lived on the Scottish West Coast Island of Jura after his wife, Eileen, died. There, he wrote his last novel at Barnhill, a cottage farmhouse he shared with his sister, chopping wood, drawing his own water, and using a motorbike for travel. He returned to England to see to the publication of 1984, and died shortly after, without seeing the book's impact. It has been in print ever since.

almost 1948

It had been pouring all day and the gulls were laughing. He could see them wheeling over the rocks. Wet to the bone, the neck of his oilskin streaming, he settled the motorbike against the roughcast wall of the stores. Someone, he knew, would be watching from inside. Here's Mr Blair with his toothbrush moustache all set to drip over the dry goods. He is cadaverously thin. Not that they ever said such things out loud, but he knew all the same. His nose started to run. A quick check found no handkerchief, not even a pocket. Only a rip, a thin line of waxed thread where the seam had been. His sister had promised to mend it and hadn't bothered. Good old Avril, dependable in a crisis. He sniffed hard, hoped for the best, and went inside. Nothing yet, Mr Blair, the big shop woman said. She was wrapping a ration of butter for a customer, a skinny sort who tilted her eyes sideways at him from under a hat. Sometimes things take a wee while.

Oh dear. Hat lady looked over sympathetically.

Can't be helped, he said. He cleared his throat, tried a smile.

I'll have Davie bring the parcel up to Barnhill, when it comes, the shop woman said. Her arms were braced on the counter now, in charge. You'll catch your death coming and going.

I'm sturdier than I look, he said, hoping for lightness, but the women exchanged a glance. Mr Blair was not well. He should not be out in this weather. They had the look of his sister, the pair of them, all motherly contempt. Most women, except the younger sort, did. I'll try in a few days, he said. Thanks all the same.

Davie was a good enough chap, but he didn't want anyone else poking through his mail. A pistol was not a usual kind of delivery and it would cause comment. He felt conspicuous enough already on the island. Since there was gin, he took one bottle and didn't ask for lemons even as a joke. Rationing this long after the war was not, had never been, funny.

Your sister's cold is better, I hope, the big one said, ringing up. And the wee boy – Richard, is it? Both women sighed. That was a nasty fall, eh?

Richard's fine, thank you, he said, irked. Not even the doctor was discreet here.

Glass, though, and stitches, the skinny one said. They're so vulnerable at that age. No idea of danger.

No, he said.

The bell rang behind him in the middle of their best wishes. One of them waved.

*

At least the rain had stopped. The sea was flat as shark skin now, cloud lifting over the scatter of islets in the harbour. Deer lowing in the distance said the threat had not gone completely, however. Out here, it never did. His calves ached with cold from the drenching of the drive down, every new twist on the track throwing up mud. Avril would pull faces when he got back, say he should never have gone out in the first place, but to hell with it. He had been out all day up a ladder with the apple trees only yesterday, then spent the evening on the hill, shooting rabbits. And he had made Richard carry them, blood dripping from their eyes and noses. Someone had to toughen the boy up. It mattered he should not be sentimental, given the way things might turn. The fate of the weak was to fall. Soon, they'd patch the barn roof and clear the garden ready for coming snow and sort out the rats in the loft. There was enough to do to keep both of them too exhausted to dwell. He had no intention of stopping the necessary physical labour of being in this place, or of laying what his sister called being a Boy Scout to rest. That was all the doctors told him – rest. Rest was not an appropriate response to encroaching lack of breath, lack of power. They had no idea what they were asking.

A shift overhead made the rain on the panniers shimmer before the light dulled again, showing the rust. All over the frame like fungus. He had carried a scythe on his back at one time, even when he drove, and it had scored the bodywork so badly the tank looked fit to split in two. It was twenty-three miles to Barnhill. If the damn thing broke down again – well, it just better not. It took three short kicks to turn over. Revving high, startling a sheep on the grass verge with the engine's sudden roar, he started the long ride back.

Past Knockrome, the road widened out into lines of rolling heather, peat and boggy turf. At the crest of the hill, the sea reappeared with its scatter of islands. Clumps of reed broke through the middle of the road, breaking what tarmac remained into a double stream. He could drive only by keeping close to the ditch, under assault by puddles and potholes, cottage loaves of dung. Today, it was slippery with leaves into the bargain, but light showed in glimpses under the heavy cloud, and it seemed he might yet manage home before another downpour.

By comparison to the journey down, this was relaxation. Rest. The doctor's word, every doctor's word, wherever he turned. *Rest.*

The last time he'd had to suffer it was at Mrs Nelson's, the day of Richard's accident. No one knew how it had happened, but the screams brought them running to find a broken chair, shattered glass and Richard, bleeding. And he'd carried him all the way from Barnhill to Mrs Nelson's, mile after sodden mile because she had the telephone, the boy bloody as a fox.

A cut to the forehead always bleeds heavy, Mrs Nelson had said. It'll not be as bad as it looks.

And soon enough the doctor had struggled up from

Craighouse with his black bag and beetled into the bathroom to start stitching. Mrs Nelson had assisted, instructing Mr Blair wait outside like an expectant father. He heard muffled moans and sobs then out she had come with Richard in her arms, five puckery black lines on his brow like a name gouged into wood. The child's eyes were wet, but he had put his arms out to be taken and fallen asleep almost immediately against the familiar scent of his father's tweeds.

The doctor was in no hurry to converse. To keep things that way, Eric offered him a cigarette.

You've been out sailing, the doctor said, nodding.

A wee bird told me.

I keep myself busy. Eric lit a match, not sure where things were leading.

You do, the doctor said. Keep mind in a place like this, word travels. He looked down on the seated man like Zeus from Olympus, big-built, bearded, determined.

Mr Blair, I feel I have to speak. I know how severe your condition is. Even if I hadn't heard, I can see for myself. Eric stiffened. The boy didn't budge.

TB isn't impressed by pluck, the doctor said. You don't fight an illness by fighting it: it gives not a hoot about your stoicism. You can't teach it a lesson. I'm telling you this very earnestly, Mr Blair. Rest. You've a book to finish. Your publisher must be anxious even if you're not. They'd tell you the same as me, I'm sure. Rest.

And Eric had nodded, silently incensed as the doctor

handed over a tube of antiseptic cream, already half-used. His nails were too clean for an islander. Suspiciously clean.

The boy will be right as rain, he said. It's you that worries me. Mrs Nelson couldn't meet his eye.

He had worked off his rage by digging peats the following day, and taken Richard along for the exercise. They had spied on plovers from the bushes then chased each other the last half-mile home. Illness was one thing: being an invalid was another. Looking back, he was sure the doctor meant well, but he was narrow. They all were. If things went on the way they were going, the war over but things unlearned, Europe would be blown to smithereens before they knew it. The bomb had changed everything. He, at least, knew it: others were turning a blind eye. If the worst happened, he could hold on in a place like this, a place too remote to pay off as a target. Here, in more senses than one, they were un-get-at-able. Doctor's advice and a so-called routine procedure had finished his wife off before her time and left father and son high and dry. Eileen. There one minute, then nothing. Nothing. Doctor's advice my arse. Whatever happened now, he had to hang on till Richard was thirteen or his sister would get hold of the boy and that would be that. Not even meaning to, just out of habit, out of a need to feel her own misery was soothed by passing it on to others. One decade. Even five – half a decade, if he got his head down. That was all he asked. In fact, he didn't ask. He'd ruddy well achieve it by means of will alone.

*

By Tarbert, the dark of the forest turned to sudden brightness. Across the bay, the sky lifted as he watched from
purple to lavender to palest blue. If the road had not been so
pitted, he would have pulled in the clutch and freewheeled
to the foot of the incline. It was glorious, this freshness after
the misery of so much rain, the sea wide and flat and calm.
Sometimes, the island and its surprises made anything
seem possible. Maybe – the thought occurred as the sun
came out, searing his eyes momentarily – maybe he should
find another wife. He was ill, granted, but not unreliable.
A man of principle. If he finished the book, and if it sold
in anything like the numbers his publisher had his fingers
crossed for, he might even – what a thought! – be rich. Avril
wouldn't like the idea one bit, but these days Avril didn't
like anything at all. He pictured Avril, his own sister, nodding agreement while the specialist pronounced him as
good as dead (*Mr Orwell, you may have less than two years at
this rate*); Avril insisting he use the pen-name to get better
treatment (*Let's face it, Eric, nobody will care unless they know
you're the Famous George Orwell. It's the only sure asset you've
got*). His hands went stiff, picturing, hearing her voice in
his head. Well, whoever the world and his ruddy sister took
him for, he wasn't giving up the ghost yet. He would finish
the book, make some money, at least get the farm running.
Now he thought of it, he'd write another will into the bargain. And another ruddy book, if he had time. Avril would
send Richard to some dreadful boarding school, even after
she knew what had happened there. *He needs more discipline,*

just the way you did. They should have been tougher. The bitch
would do it out of spite. The motorbike was bouncing over
shale now, shaking him down to his bones. She wasn't
getting Richard. One way or another, he'd make damned
sure. It wasn't impossible to find a wife who'd sort things
out afterwards the way he wanted. The way he insisted.
After the war, it was easy to find women who'd marry first
chance they got.

The wind was in his eyes.

Eric never wept, not even for Eileen, but from time to
time, his eyes watered. He rubbed them with his left cuff as
the bike scudded on. Great walls of layered rock were rising
on either side obscuring the fields. Then, as he began the
climb out of the valley, a crack rang out, a sound like the sky
opening. At the same moment, the bike slid sharply sideways, the engine revving wildly as he rolled his grip on the
handlebars. He was aware of the ditch to his left, the solid
rock veering far too close, the crack of gunfire again, again
as something fluttered overhead. The machine cobbled as
he struggled to regain control, lost. It was then, as the bike
tipped past the point of stability, he saw a face. Long and
greyish, watching from the bracken, its eyes steady. The
engine cut sharply as the machine crashed down onto the
heather, Eric drawing back by instinctive sleight. Barely
upright, he focused on the bracken, then wheeled, checking afresh, the sound of his own heart dinning in his ears.
Now, however, with the light shifted and his gaze still, he
saw the face was nothing. Mere rock, a bare patch showing

pale against the terracotta ferns. Maybe there had been no
face at all, just fear. Surprise. A trick of the light. He keeled
forward, breathed deep and coughed till he almost retched.
Not a face, he told himself, choking. No assassin, no accuser.
It was no one at all.

Miraculously, the gin was unbroken, the bike in no worse
shape than before. No one, so far as he was aware, had seen
his fall but the pheasants. And they were stupid. Stupid
birds with no survival instinct. Even so, people shot them.
It seemed poor sport. Another burst of gunfire sounded;
distant wings, flailing. He wiped his mouth. The cloth of his
trousers near the knee was torn, the flesh beneath seeping
slightly. Other than that, he was unscathed. He allowed his
shoulders to drop, almost smiled. He was still here. He was,
after a fashion, fine.

The bike started first boot. Ahead was the way to
Ardlussa. Tonight, he thought, staring ahead, he'd take
Richard out and they'd hunt rats in the barn with hammers.
A hammer trained a neat mind, an accurate eye, at least till
the parcel arrived. Things would be better when the Luger
came. Meanwhile, they'd manage.

Ravens wheeled in a nearby field, cawing. He had his
book to finish, the farm to attend to, his son to raise. There
were, in the real world, no alternatives. He lifted his feet
and descended, roaring, into the home stretch.

that was then, this is now (2)

Where's Claire?

Claire sits in front of the tv. On the screen, dots hoach and recompose themselves, throw different-coloured shapes onto her face that make her look diseased. She's not. She's forty-seven today, two glasses of wine and Ribena to the wind, and smiling. The tv makes the face of a man out of pixels, his features fading and remaking themselves, his hair growing, shortening again, his skin getting younger, older, then back the way it was before. It changes umpteen times before he melts completely and a car surfaces out of the digital chaos: big expensive black car with a walnut dashboard and leather upholstery, Eric Clapton playing either in the background or on its concealed surround-sound bass-boosted stereo. It goes round on a podium, gleaming like an American football helmet, showing itself off, and Eric croons like he's in love with it, like he wants to shin up to its balcony and throw it a rose.

She's been through the other channels. Football, some

show about a serial killer who's really a good guy deep
down and a bunch of male and female suits talking London
politics and the importance of not taxing high-earners
because the trickle-down effect is our best hope.

The adverts were definitely the best. Another one comes
on, about tampons giving you freedom to be *Anyone You
Choose*. Claire is not impressed. She's not interested. She's
not even awake. Little snores, animal puffs and wheezes,
escape from her nose and mouth. In one open hand, she's
holding a fire engine. There's another one beside her, near
her hip. There is a wooden policeman, a furry dinosaur,
six different rally cars, bits of torn paper, a pen, an electric
ball, displaced rubber shapes from an absent game and a
knitted snake in stripes of whatever was left at the bottom
of the wool box. A torch, still on, shines out from under
the settee. A serving spoon. One sock. Then the tampons
finish and some game show with sex jokes takes over.
The best bit is the titles: the rest is people throwing water
at each other, laughing at the word *penis* and making out
it's funny. It's not. It's stupid. They are behaving like kids'
tv presenters only it's after the watershed so there's no
excuse. Claire would have liked the graphics for the car
advert. She used to be in advertising. She was good at it.
She would have liked the car too, sometimes misses the
fancy four-door that used to be her own, but right now, it
doesn't matter. It doesn't signify. Claire is making drool
blots on the cushion under her cheek, Rorschach prints.

Dreaming the dreams of the blessed, barely able to believe this life she refused to consider for so many years is finally hers, Claire is deeper in love than she's ever been. Out cold.

fine day

I don't love you any more.

Her knees hurt and her head was racing. Go on, say it. But he didn't. He kept sitting in front of the fire, a bright halo flickering behind his head, the cigarette between his fingers ghosting smoke over one eye. It would be a relief if he just went for it, spat things out straight for once; spoke in terms that were not bloodless. But he didn't. His language was strictly impersonal, tight-arsed counselling mode.

It's ok for people to want different things, he said. It's ok.

Sure, she said. It's hunky bloody dory.

Don't be like that, he said. It's not like you.

No, she said. It's not.

His face in the reflection of the flames made him look soft but his tone gave him away. He wanted no truck with contradiction. *Agree with me or you are unreasonable.* Katrin rolled her eyes at never being able to deal with this, somehow. It was Katrin-proof. She tried not to feel so terrible.

Katrin, he sighed. Kat.

Once, that had been his pet name for her, something to

use in bed or especially delighted by his luck they were together: these days, it meant he was barely holding on to civility. Hearing it made her queasy.

It's ok for two people to grow in different directions. He exhaled slowly. It's ok to change, to make a mature decision – she snorted – *a mature decision* to move on. It's the civilised thing to do.

Well, she said. Got me there, bang to rights. Her voice cracked. Can't argue with the *how-to-be-civilised* fucking manual.

But sarcasm was no match for long-suffering condescension. He had the upper hand and they both knew it. Swear, weep, show passion of any kind, and the game was up. It was his training, she supposed: Murray could wrong-foot a seminar group of thirty when he had to. He wasn't going to weaken for her. He blew a smoke ring, poised as Garbo. Katrin watched the kiss of his breath as he let it go, felt something with long, desperate fingers squirming in the barrel of her chest. It hurt badly.

Let's be reasonable, he said, his voice distant, as though he was talking from a different planet through an intercom; it's not the fifties. There's no call for shame. We needn't classify this as failure.

No, she said, flat. It's not even called *separation* any more. It's called *moving on* or *redefining one's priorities* or *conscious uncoupling* god help us and it's all perfectly ok. She swallowed hard, hoping to god she wouldn't cry and infuriate him. But is it still ok if they have children?

Jesus Katrin, he said. She heard him snort, knock back what was left of his whisky. It's all about guilt for you, isn't it? And we have only *one*. One child. Which other children are you factoring in?

Own goal. At least she hadn't used the word *selfish*. The s-word made him walk out mid-sentence last time – three days with no contact. He wasn't pleased, though. Mentioning their son was dragging Danny into it and joint decisions regarding Danny were high on Murray's list of unsayables. *Emotional blackmail* he called it: trying to get him roped in on a discussion about how they should act as a pair for at least this was *questioning his sincerity*, his trump card in a game of *smug*. He might point out that as an educator, he needed no lectures on child welfare from *her*. She might benefit from a short, sharp course on the importance of strong male role models for boys and how smothering mothers could be. Also he was a busy man. A trick to pin him down to schedules and having to ask her fucking permission was not only unworkable but unacceptable. *As well she knew.*

Sarcasm would at least be engagement, but he was above that kind of thing, by and large. He did ice-cold. He did it because it worked. Because it froze her out. He took another draw and stayed put, expressionless. Katrin looked into the fire behind him, wondering when she had last checked the real-effect coals, whether the jets needed servicing, why it was always her that wondered these things. All this *being civilised* hokum was costing fortunes in metered units.

Well, he said eventually. He stood, flexing his knees. I'll get my stuff. Are you – you know? Ok?

For a dreadful moment, Katrin felt she might throw back her head and scream with grief and impotence. She didn't. She just stared. She looked up at him as though she wished his ribcage would implode, just crush in on itself from sheer narcissism. Say it say it, she thought, her eyes searing. For once, just cut to the chase. After eight years, eight years of Murray looking pained, so intricately, unspecifically pained if she suggested anything so commonplace as talking about what made him so troubled; five of them, the five since she had fallen pregnant, in fact, spent on a relay of Murray wandering off to *reassess his needs* or *find his space* or – his favourite – *to be without having to explain himself.* And all that time, she had opted for wide berths, patience and the doleful hope that Danny wouldn't learn something fucked-up from the whole business. Now here they were again, nothing ventured, nothing won, Murray rising to his feet and asking if *she* was ok. *I want to leave, Katrin.* Or *Danny needs more than this, Katrin.* Even *Tell you what, Katrin, just count me out, it's over* – they would be ok. They were not, however, on offer. Murray needed the freedom to flit in and out of lives as though they were incidental train platforms between his journey to himself. He was also looking at her.

Cab, he said. I need a cab.

For a moment she wondered if he was telling her to call one for him, caught herself in time to avoid the automatic response. If he'd had enough, she knew how he felt.

He stopped momentarily at the door, singling out a slim volume of Nietzsche from the bookshelf, slipping it into a pocket as though he had no idea it wasn't his. She heard him poke numbers into the hall phone, the tune signalling a local firm. He hadn't said where he was spending the night this time. This time, he hadn't said lots of things. A newspaper, probably pinched from the college staffroom, lay on the rug, its tv schedules in neat, domestic columns. The word *Butterfly* loomed blackly near a picture of a politician whose wife had left him. The headline read *No Comment*.

So. The voice was frighteningly close. Murray was standing near right behind her when she turned, looked up. He had his coat on, his scarf knotted in preparation for the lousy weather outside. I'm off.

He stubbed the last of the cigarette, making a concertina on the tray that glittered redly, refusing to go out. Then slowly, like a film loop rerunning itself, a grainy final footage of a now-dead actor, he knelt back down and looked at her. His jaw was taut and perfect, lit with flame. Ashamed of her uselessness, Katrin stood quickly and went out into the hallway. His suitcase was leaning against the wall, waiting. She had no idea when he had packed it, that it was heading off with him too. Something new. A corner of his best dress shirt poked out between the case lid and its lower jaw, and she wondered, helpless, what on earth he needed that for. His dress shirt, for crying out loud. What else was he taking and not, not this time, coming back to fetch? At that moment, a horn sounded and Murray hared in from the living room, almost colliding with her back.

Sorry, he said, the way he might to a stranger in a shopping mall. Didn't see you.

He was reaching for the bag, straightening, taking a half-step towards her as though offering an embrace, then changed his mind abruptly and opened the door instead. Cold knifed in as he paused on the top step, his eyes on her mouth, her ear, her wedding ring.

I love you, he said. He turned up his collar, preparing for the rain, the waiting taxi. Don't ever forget that, Katrin. I really do.

And the door banged shut.

Shut.

She picked two cartons of apple juice, the kind with straws, from the fridge. A packet of crisps, two wee boxes of raisins, slices of brown bread sealed with peanut butter and cut into squares the size of stamps. No fresh fruit – there was never enough fresh fruit – but this would do. A midnight feast didn't have to be fancy. Last, she put a toy car into her pocket, just in case, and headed upstairs.

His room was thick, the darkness filled with the soft purr of his breathing. She said nothing, just listened. Then something about her being there, a shift in the texture of the air, made him wake. She heard the covers ruffle, knew he was sitting up in the pitch black, blinking, so warm you could cook eggs on him. He didn't speak, just reached out knowing she'd be there, sure she'd be reaching back. His little body was solid, dependable, the way it always was. She heard him rub his eyes, his fist twisting against his cotton pyjama sleeve. All she had to do was lift. She blew into his hair for the pleasure of hearing that snuffling noise he made, a snort of pleasure in the dark. We're sharing a joke, she thought, almost shocked. He was nuzzling against her without knowing what had hit him, what might hit either of them, yet. What might one day have to be explained with no solid explanation. Whatever it was, Katrin would have to be ready. That was her job. It was important to explain. She winched Danny closer, taking his weight.

You used to be an octopus after your bath, she said. Her voice was catching. You waved your legs like this.

She flexed one of his knees, making his leg flop like something filleted. His chest was smooth as an unripe plum, a boy emerging from the folds of baby fat. She stroked his ankle, his shin, the hard length of bone beneath. Milk did this, she thought. Her breasts made bones, male bones. Danny wriggled, restless. He had no interest in the story of his baby self. She cupped the peachy handfuls of his bottom and squeezed.

Ok, Danny. Cmon. You and me.

Where? he said, rubbing his eyes.

The opera, she said. We're going to the opera.

So. The night Murray left, the night Danny's daddy made his final exit without even knowing it himself, they watched *Madam Butterfly*. The chorus milling by the time they found the channel, waiting for Cio Cio San, the bought wife, the too-serious minded, the too credulous, to arrive. From the crook of his mother's arm, Danny stared at the colours, the sprays of stage blossoms, the splays of fans. Katrin gave him a sandwich.

Who's that? he said, chewing. Butterfly was coming on, fragile and wilfully optimistic.

Butterfly, Katrin whispered. She's getting married.

Danny stared. What for?

That was a hard one. Well, Katrin tried, that man wants a wife. See? Pinkerton. He's American and she's not. She's poor. Her uncle is angry.

Oh, he said. She gave him a carton. He sucked, watching the Bonze cursing his niece for dishonouring the family while the chorus bristled with shame.

Why are they singing?

They do that instead of talking, she said. It makes it special.

Danny looked up at her, his mouth moved round the straw, then watched without more questions. By the time the orchestra ebbed into *One Fine Day*, he was out for the count, the fallen carton on his lap. Through the swoop and swallow-dive of Butterfly asserting for sure that Pinkerton was coming home, Katrin wept without relief. Everyone did it, she thought, they waited for this terrible, beautiful moment: Butterfly serving herself up like beef on the bone, refusing to grasp the truth. Meanwhile, through the roaring and heart-wrenching, a little boy sat quiet on the edge of the set. There he was, now Katrin looked, the tiny child actor – they were always tiny – playing Butterfly and Pinkerton's son. He toyed with a fallen fan, good as gold. Then the camera lost interest, slid back to the soprano. *I know*, she sang, the whole audience knowing the opposite, *I know he will return.* When she knew the lie for what it was and the ceremonial sword appeared, glittering under the stage lights, Katrin reached for the remote, flicked.

What happened next was a miracle: a snip of footage on the late-night news. A middle-aged man, it said, had lifted a car, saving the life of a teenage boy near Wakefield. The newsreader looked urbane and amused, not astounded. Jerky footage showed the man, red-faced and middle-aged, his hands under the radiator grille. And the car lifting. Not much, but enough. The car lifting, the dark shape of a boy, pulling free. They showed it twice, then ran an interview. He was not a hero, he said. You just did what you had to. You never knew what that was till you tried. Then the news-reader smiled and wished everyone goodnight. Closing feel-good story. Incidental. Light. When the weatherman arrived, chirpy in front of a bright blue sky, Katrin switched off the tv altogether. Bits of scattered picnic littered the rug, a single butter knife. Even when she twisted to move it out of harm's way, Danny didn't wake. She kissed his forehead for the feel of his skin on hers, thought briefly of Murray, scudding through the dark to godknew where. Wherever he was headed, he'd be ok. But Danny was the centre of the picture now. *Un bel dì, vedremo levarsi un fil di fumo.* In her by-numbers Italian accent, understanding it only as sound, she sang to her son's closed lids, his oblivious, perfect face. And tomorrow she'd phone a locksmith. It was, she thought, a mature decision to move on. What she knew now she knew for sure. They'd get by. Not looking back. They might even bloom.

greek

Switch off the ignition and the shuddering dies. There is only the sound of the sea.

The first time we met, he was with someone else. I bust into the wrong room in the British Museum looking for first-century seal-stones of the type once used in intimate correspondence by the Hellenes and there he was, side on with his lips swathed round some dark-rooted blond guy's face like a catfish sucking an aquarium wall. I slipped away with my notebook hoping they hadn't noticed I'd dropped my pen but half-way down the stairwell I heard footfalls. And there he was, leaning over the banister from two floors up, grinning like bones. He magicked a little linen square from somewhere, blew his nose elegantly and put the square away in one smooth gesture without taking his eyes off me. *The least you should do when you walk in on someone's private life is say hello, don't you think?*

One step at a time, like an actor, he descended, a faint dusting of something showing on his coat lapels when we were level, like icing sugar. Snow.

You should chill out more, he said.

His accent made me feel British, possessed of anally retentive vowels.

Say hi, he said. He took a long, deep breath, bit his teeth together with a click. Say hi. Say hi to Ike.

Nine months later, stoned, we got married and the bloke with the roots didn't show. We'd been holed up in Ike's flat, drinking and having too much sex and laughing at nothing to think straight. I hadn't seen my own digs for months, done no research. I didn't care.

I walked barefoot into the registry office, all turquoise dress and fish-scale eyeshadow, crying from sheer exhaustion. He was wearing lipstick.

I can't take you anywhere, he said, dabbing my tears away with the tail end of his sleeveless shirt as the registrar explained the binding nature of the commitment we were about to undertake. You're a fucking liability.

His English was impeccable, flecked with mica. I all but swooned. As I Will Survive played low in the background, he slipped a ring he'd made himself from copper wire and gold leaf on my finger and we were a breeding pair. To celebrate, we went straight back to his flat with the people we hardly knew, the owner of Ken's Authentic Kebabs at the corner of the street and his grown-up daughter in a nice dress scented with allspice, and shared out the Marks and Spencer salmon rolls, prawn crackers and fizz we'd got by way of a wedding feast. We clinked glasses. We laughed. Turtle doves.

Nothing was different to start with, just more intense. We read to each other from random books picked up in street markets, left the radio on all the time and fiddled with the channels, talked and fucked like rabbits. Ike stopping any of this to sleep was optional. He just kept going all the time, talking to himself if I was fading. I'd wake up sometimes on the living room carpet, mascara streaked around my eyes and find a note: *have fun x Ike* and crisp bags, digestives, crusts of bread. Whatever it was he did – services he called it, bit of dealing in the city – it paid the rent after a fashion, or I assumed it did because I didn't and we were still there. The toilet was scribbled over with pictograms, his and mine, from trips where we had chosen to sit for a long time in there just for the chance to think, words written backwards, calculus, drawings of wings. DON'T LOOK DOWN – one read – IT WILL ONLY MAKE YOU DIZZY. It must be his I thought, I would remember if I'd written that. It has to be his. It was a while before I found the proof, his name, after a fashion, scratched out in archaic script into the bathroom plaster: Ἴκ-αρ-ος. Ike-are-us.

Before long, a little blue sports car arrived in the parking bay. He couldn't drive.

I'm only thinking of you, he said. You need to get out more. Who's it for, baby? Who could it be for?

He swung the keys from one finger, looked at me like I was six.

Give me a lift to show you're pleased. Smiling that smile

that smacked me senseless every time. Come on, Helen. Be a mensch.

Where did you get the money? I said.

Secret, he said. All the best surprises are. I'm Greek – the art of surprise is our specialism. He breathed into my hair. It's what we do. Isn't that what you fell for, Helen? Little bit of reckless? He put his finger in my mouth, took it back, licked the space between the roots of my digits with his tongue till my spine shifted. Isn't that exactly what you like?

It was crabs that broke the camel's back. I'm fine, he said. I'm careful. Look, I'm not angry but it must be something you're doing. Just get it seen to.

I said I couldn't have caught as much as a cold from someone else right now and he shrugged.

Those guys at the library. They catch all sorts from those ancient old books you like. You should shower when you come back. Let's not blame. You should sleep in the spare room till you're clear, ok?

Relate. One-hour appointment. Forty quid.

He flirted with their counsellor and undid his shirt buttons, showing off a brand-new Tiffany chain. Outside, away from the door where nobody could hear, I snapped.

You're out of control, Ike, I said, my knuckles white. You take nothing seriously.

Fine, he said. He opened the car door and jumped ship,

leaving me stuck on a red. If that's how you feel. Did I hear tears in his voice, a catch? I've given this my best shot. Pigeons parted for him, feathers scattering as he hared for a cab. Tonight just sleep in the fucking car.

It dawned on me he meant I had no keys. I could picture them in the fruit bowl where the figs used to be. Maybe he was planning to shut me out. Temporarily, at least, I was homeless. I circled. I cried. I couldn't find him.

I came here.

Here.

This was where he brought me that first night to show me the vista. It's the edge of the world, he whispered. We're on the high wire. Don't look down.

We were too near to see how sheer the drop was anyway, but I could hear the boom and echo, the shrill of gulls. He made love to me on the thin strip of verge and I was exhilarated. Like I was flying.

Now what I see is the interminable ocean, a concrete wall together with the sky, the crumbling brink. I get out of the car and, hand above my eyes, cast for signs. Something glints on the opposite headland, a torch maybe, a shape through the smirr that could be a man. I take my ring off, hold it up to the watery sun, signal back. Me and my wedding ring and the edge of the world. Something has to give. One of the two. Me or my wedding ring.

My toes curl on shale.

*

The man on the far hill opens out like a crucifix or a bird and the knowledge I have not had a period for months now coils like a worm beneath my abdomen. Fleetingly, I wonder what happened to root boy. His two colours of hair.

Gnôthi seautón. He shouts. *Know thyself.* You're a waste of fucking space.

It's true. I am. Look down, I think. My head is spinning. My stomach butterflies. Is it mine? Or that of another, smaller creature? I didn't sign up for this.

He spreads his arms wider.

Me and the ring: the precipice. Within the realms of possibility, an accidental new life nourished on coke and alcohol that could pin me to this stranger for the rest of my life. Our lives. Something has to give.

There's only one fair choice.

The sound of the sea.

Ike, shrieking.

Working in another country, having witnessed some kind of unprovoked attack in a park just off a big white art gallery that same afternoon, I read a newspaper story about a mother of two who killed her three-year-old daughter and husband in their home. The woman's other daughter, aged eight, was in intensive care at a local hospital with severe head injuries following a fall. The woman, who was said to suffer from acute schizophrenia, attended the same hospital for injuries to her hands before being released into police custody. Something about the story seemed familiar and it stayed with me.

turned

Mornings were pink and the afternoons were green and brown. Evening colours were harder to define. Evening colours were bruised and shifting. They were a colour all right, but no colour with a name. Nothing I could define.

It's the reaching out.

It's always the reaching out that does it.

The same, same dream, same detail, same accident. Accidents. And it starts with waking. This is the final act. It starts

now.

The room is full of moonlight. He isn't there.

The unfocused interior and broken stillness ringing round the room. It's her old bedroom – the scent of powdery wallpaper thick enough to touch. Fishing up from the safety of sleep is never pleasant. After the freedom of weightless absence, the heaviness of the body is oppressive, dragging on the bones. There are eyelids to recall, the awkwardness and reluctance of the mechanism, optic nerves tugging against their moorings. All of it hurts. This place is undeniable now. It keeps coming back. It always does. This room. It is full of moonlight. The rim of the bed electric blue from the artificial brightness beyond the curtain. Nobody ever closes them. That could mean winter, it might be winter with no expectation of early dawn. These swollen ellipses overhead, rubbing against the ceiling surreptitiously, are balloons. Party leftovers. They're nosing the pale plaster up there like fish kissing the surface of a tank, needing to feed. This is a deep-sea tank. You are at the bottom.

The air clings, the time of night turning her arms to underwater grey. But for all that, the room is not chill. Not at all. The blankets are thick, the bed reassuringly solid. There are animals, toys perhaps, face down in the corners of the carpet, a bundle of cast-off clothing splayed over a chair: dungarees, a round-collared shirt, socks edged with lace. Nearby are a pair of sandals, one like a wind-break on its side. The casts of toes, a shoreline, are outlined in dye on the white tips of their soles. Her toes. A long time ago perhaps, but hers. That scent on the shirred cotton would be hers too if she bothered to get up and check, but there's no real need. Closing her eyes tight is all it takes to recall the cool of the cloth, the awkwardnesses of those buckles, buttons, straps. Hands not her own have smoothed those surfaces over no breasts at all, hauled her backwards from the oncoming traffic by those straps. They are thin straps and leave marks, a red blood harness on a baby chest. Those pencils on the desk carry imprints of milk-teeth. Elsewhere, over the desk, are bears. Frieze. That's her mother's word: frieze, but it's got nothing to do with cold. It means BEARS, groups of threes, etched on the memory from repeated watching, their picnic scattered on the painted grass, stalking each other across the facing wall in awful repetitions with the letter B. After all this time the bears seem no closer to whatever it is they're chasing beyond the bounds of the paper rim.

They'll never catch it now. They show no disappointment. Everything real is off the edge of where they are, but they haven't a clue. Not like you, not at all. You're right here, right now and everything is just as it should be. There are no such things as ghosts, no invisible people. Dark places, perhaps, things that moan beneath the bed at night, shapes moving behind mirrors, but no invisible people. There is only the wind and the roof, the joists settling. There are only Mother and Father and Angela, and they're here too. Look, pinned behind glass over the headboard in deep gilt frames. Only a photograph, black and white, their true colours having no way of being recorded in those days but that's who they are, so like themselves, you can almost hear them.

Look, she said. I could cut off my fingers and you'd think it was your due. Her hands are red with beetroot. Yes, he said. His face was one picture, not shifting. I could cut off all my fingers, she said, and pile them on a plate. Her knuckles dripped on the lino, audible. She had lipstick on her teeth.

A rag doll, hair in ribbons, sits under the picture, throwing a shadow of itself against the door. Beneath that shadow is a picture of you with your name on it, handwritten in green crayon. Your name your name. Your name. Before you can think what it is, a pain in your head becomes sharper, sore as cutting. All this remembering, this trying to retain. No matter what, that is what you have to do right now, to think and remember.

Whose baby hands are these? Whose?

These are your hands spread like paste against the dark billows of the quilt.

That's the sound of blood, coursing.

Who are you? Who's my favourite girl?

You are inside your own self and this is your room.

Your name. Your name is

The curtains are open, showing grainy clouds, an edge of a full moon shedding light like a faulty shower. It sprinkles the little room finely, leaves nothing untouched. Moonlight. Light from the Moon. From so far away, it's cold by the time it reaches. Now it shows everything in its drowned, grey glow. That's what woke you, then, this one forgotten courtesy. No one had pulled the curtains and shut out the Moon. If she does it herself, however, and quickly enough, she might get back to sleep and wake up somewhere else. The prospect is so enticing, so near, it's irresistible. Moving, she braces her hands against the edge of the mattress and swings her legs to the floor. The boards are varnished and cold; they fleck her soles with dust. The window, however, is clean. It's clean enough not to be there at all, the sill icy as metal. *Don't look.* She knows she shouldn't. *Don't look outside.* She touches it anyway, the heat of her hand spreading on the perishing glass. She looks *don't look don't look* outside.

Under this very window, faintly veiled, a tight cluster of equidistant bushes appears. It is rimmed by strips of crew-cut lawn, a border of granite pebbles. The dog-bark sound of snipping gets louder. Maybe it was always there. But this is not what matters. What matters is the woman. That coat, the set of those raised arms. Her back is to you, and you cannot see her face, but you know all the same. There is no one else it can be.

You might try to kill us all one day, she said; how would I protect myself? There were pink flowers behind her on the sill, threatening to shed. I know that look, she said, roaring. I know what's in your pocket. His arms warm on either side, braced your face and shoulders. The smell of wool from his jumper, the bottle rattling pills in his hand.

In the gardens beneath, my mother is pruning roses. Pyres of branches build about her boots, more falling as you watch. But for this bitten hacking, the steady clip of her secateurs, there is silence. And you think. You cannot help yourself. All that green wood, cloying at her ankles. Sap smokes in a fire. Joan of Arc refusing to burn. It would take a long, long time. Mother knows nothing of what you are thinking, however; she never does. She knows only the next incision. She is still, intent, her muscles flexing under those green rubber gloves. At her neck she wears a blouse with a schoolgirl collar, a collar so white, her head shows jet above it. The slash of wrist between the gauntlet cuff and the dark sleeve of her coat is pallid as mushroom; in this light, almost lavender. You watch it for some time, checking for a pulse. Mother merely works on. Keep watching, notice with some pride your mother's deftness, the proof of years of practice slicing godknows what: the young stems present her with no difficulty at all. Even when no more heads remain, she will cut on. The plant will be tamed, her feet snowed under with shorn blooms. The sound of cutting rings clean enough to sharpen teeth. A baby, naked on the grass beside her has its eyes wide open, but Mother needs nothing else. Out here, working, though she called your name, she does not need you. Maybe there is nothing to fear after all.

Another head falls, rolls on the freshly sliced earth. And it occurs then, in the moment of its rocking, the petals still clustered about the heart, she might know that you are watching. She might suspect, turn, see. The baby with the wide eyes isn't moving. Its hands look broken on their stems. Perhaps it's a doll. But it's not. It's not. Press the pane with your fingertips. There is something else, something yet to be faced. Past the butchered bushes, the rich dankness of the soil beds, there is something else to understand. That's when you see his arm, languishing on the fallen leaves, the unnatural twist of it, splayed.

Turn. Try to breathe and turn. Turn.

Someone is running. You hear it clearly. Grass, rushes, clutches of fern move sharply past. Then trees. Further off, rolling tangles of bracken, barbed wires of bramble, crawling moss. Thickets of weed rear from and recede into a dark so deep, what little light remains seems sucked towards it. It looks damp, stifling; a place where not even a cry for help would penetrate. No one could live out there, you think, and anything might hide. While the breath pushes at your ribcage, you pause, knowing it is not the thing to do. You should keep moving, keep running. Over your shoulder, the place you are leaving, maybe forever, shows the stock-still earth, the bloomless beds. There are the bundles of branches, one fallen frog-green glove. A knife. Mother is no longer beside the roses, but elsewhere, invisible and searching. You know she is searching, and who she is searching for is anyone's guess. That she will find you have no doubt. This is no longer asleep, the safety behind your own eyelids: you're here for sure on the pebble border, afraid to draw attention by calling his name. Those are your toes curling over the white stones, that sound is your heart, drumming. The smell of mulch and recent spading is overwhelming and far too close. A light rip like tearing cloth makes you turn. Turn. Turn.

She's not herself, he said. But she loves you. Look at the flowers. Who d'you think they're for? She grows you those lovely flowers.

The pain in your chest sears, your eyes run. But not

enough to miss what's coming. Even through the rain
it's clear. Something moving. Here it comes: a tumulus of
restless earth struggling upward through the soil, inching
closer. Watch it come, pause as though catching its breath,
begin again. Six feet away, the movement is close enough
to see in detail, a seethe and a slump like something buried
but not dead yet, struggling beneath the layer of grass. Keep
watching as it stretches a last time, then the grass begins to
tear. Gently, a tiny O appears. The O widens to the size of
a green cat's yawn. Listen. You can hear the sound of roots
parting, tearing like animal sinew. Twigs and stems of ivy
are falling into the hole-mouth now, its edges fattening out
to the breadth of a shark-mouth. And here you are in this
shifting, unkent garden, bare feet, nails turning blue. A
scent of burning carries on a drift of night-stock, catching
the back of the throat but there is no sign of Mother, none.
Not yet. Another tumulus noses from the forest now, a live
thing burrowing closer across the lawn. You should not
wait to see more. Run. Run. Run through trees, thicket, clots
of grass; under branches and low-hanging vine; through
blackness so complete you may as well be floating. Beneath
your naked feet, the leaves of decades gust a thick, aromatic
scent, and unseen things, little pulses of life, shift out of
range of your vision. But you go on nonetheless, clearing
fallen logs and unidentifiable debris, sunken arms of long-
dead wood, knowing the running is all that matters. The
grass underfoot relaxes too, seems lusher. It stretches under
the soles. Tempting to let the shoulders fall, breathe more

deeply, agree that in the dark is safety. Too late. Only on its edge does the cloud lift enough, only on the edge do the eyes become accustomed enough and there is the maw, a strew of roots ineptly covering the pit. In the split second before falling, you recall Mother's neat cotton collar, the lilac cast of her skin. And falling, tearing at the edge of the hollow you think you hear someone call your name. A woman's voice. Whatever you do don't answer. Your. Name. Your

name.

Everything stops.

Dead.

There's no thud, no crushing pain. Nothing hurts but your jaw, clenched for the impact that does not come. Open your eyes slowly and there is merely half-light, a mist curled on flat, red-packed earth. No spikes, no thorns, no obvious trap; only this depth, the steepness of the sides, a hole overhead. From here it shows perfectly round, a needle pointing where you cannot go. *Home.* Huge clouds make ghosts in the sky. The road is up there, the voice that called your name. But maybe that is illusion too. Maybe everything was. And this is your true beginning. *Home.* Stroke the sticky sides of the pit with soft-nailed fingers, hear loose pockets of its substance slither and drop. Slick fibres touch your back, tickle your neck like antennae. These legs will serve, tucked under you like rockers, the firm breadth of these thighs. Your fingers are sinuous, the veins showing in the wrists. If you had a mirror, you might see your own heartbeat, so thin is this blood-warm skin. For now, though, the sides of the pit stretch high and steep, a snake coils at your knees. The floor is beating. The whole pit glows pink as a gullet. Home. Now it begins, slowly and deliberately, a steady flexing of muscle. Press back against the pit-side, its contracting power. Tell yourself splendid lies.

And maybe you will sleep now.

Maybe when you wake it will all have been a mistake.

You will be on the surface again, grown, your feet sensibly shod and ready for the road. Maybe you will walk into a clearing and see a bend appear. You will turn it, and he will appear. He will be some way off still, but his smile will be discernible. And despite this tiredness, this terrible heaviness that might be a heart, you will reach out then. You will reach as though your lungs might burst towards his embrace. The sides shudder, tighten. There is no going back.

He pulled aside the top sheet and smiled. You'd never get up in the morning if I didn't wake you. Scatter of teddy bears, plastic figurines. Sleeping Beauty, he said. Sleepyhead.

Father, your heart says, testing. I could cut off my fingers for you. Do you imagine you can change things this time, this time?

The sides heave. Reach up. Turn and prepare. He is waiting out there, knowing nothing. Reach. Reach and turn.

And the reaching
  the reaching

  the room is full of

    it is full

      full

gold

Blister cushions
Small flashlight
Signal mirror
Compass

She should write it down. A note, a message; something clear and clean. He would want to know.

The first time it appeared, she understood what had happened, but did not know what to think. By the second and third, the pattern was clear, but waiting even a little longer would show she had been contained enough to offer some kind of testimony. And by the fifth day, she was ready. After the morning's now usual ritual, she sat up inside the sleeping bag, folded the pillow, and reached for the notebook Charlie had given her, still clean inside its plastic case. The pen still loaded with ink. All she had to do was open a fresh page. Then write it out in simple language. One careful letter at a time.

Every morning now for close on five days, the sun comes to meet me. It filters through the roof vent in a single shaft of light. And turns my hands to gold.

Grace was never *flesh-colour*. Then neither was anyone else. *Flesh-colour* was a watery pink-brown that existed in crayons and hosiery, not human beings. Nobody was *one colour*, whatever data-collection surveys thought: human skin had varied dramatically over time and migration, but human beings were a sole lineage; every last one of us some shade of brownish, the same family. What the questionnaire hoped to illuminate was anyone's guess. Admittedly, Grace ticked the *white* box when compelled, but not without irritation. Arguing with a piece of paper was worse than a waste of time and effort, it was nuts. Her hostility to official questionnaires, however, persisted.

Looking back, that rage could have been better used. She had not written letters to the Home Office, the local press, certainly never marched under a banner: she had kept it to herself. No one explained that inner turmoil and alienation in general might have been stoked by the shifts of adolescence. Her preparation for what her mother called *changes* had been a brief shopping trip for extra underwear, a pack of sanitary towels, and unexplained advice to *be careful*. Puzzled but dutiful, Grace chose to be careful about as much as possible, but her capacity to face down problems got in the way. The best part of adolescence, which made up for all the rest, was the trick of being able to fall asleep as soon as her head hit the pillow: from fully alert to out-for-the-count in seconds was all bene- fits. Now, still struggling through the menopause, only trazodone offered anything like it. Waking up through the night, not once but serially, was the norm of her late fifties. And every time she woke, her head, undistracted in the dark, filled with the same list of fears: melting ice caps, extinctions of species, choked oceans, displaced people, drowning children and the cracking open of the whole world for shale gas. So far, her seventh decade had offered joint pain (the thumb-joints, my god, the random ratchet- ing of her thumb-joints), minimal hearing loss, forgetting the ends of sentences, and grief-stricken dreams about the slow death of the planet. And in these things, indeed in the whole of her assiduously pared-back life, she was, and knew it, luckier than most.

It wasn't a great start. Her mother, Barbara, having blind- eyed a pregnancy, was found out by relentless morning sickness and sent by her parents to an Evangelical Home for Unmarried Mothers lest the neighbours find out and shame kill them. Before things went wrong, however, Barbara had been to the pictures more than once, and was struck dumb by pallid, perfect, open-faced Grace Kelly in the film *High Noon*. A bit part, but unforgettable for its freshness: a woman who looked like sunlight. And when her child arrived, its tiny face luminous in the low-lit ward at 4 a.m. with two other girls exactly like Barbara peering anxiously inside from the open corridor, its name seemed obvious. *Grace*. It arrived in the moment, exactly when needed and not before. As if it had been planned all along. As if this child had meant to be kept all along and not handed over to the Salvation Army or indeed anyone at all who looked like they might take her somewhere far away. Premature, underweight, illegitimate, the most pasty-faced baby anyone had ever seen was given a film-star name and her mother's immediate change of heart, almost on sight. A name that no one would shorten, distort or make fun of. She called her *Grace*.

Grace retained no memories of early childhood, and assumed that to be normal. Just as she assumed being alone looking out of the window while mum was out working was normal from the age of four. Her primary schooling was unremarkable save that when some mothers or grand-mothers came to pick up her classmates to take them home at the end of the day, she stayed on with one other in an ante-room with colouring books till someone picked them up an hour later. It was nothing personal: just how it was. Grace passed an exam that let her go on to grammar school, where some of the teachers, the men most of all, seemed still in recovery from the war. The classrooms were bigger and the teachers, shell-shocked or not, wore scraggy gowns, like teachers in a comic book. Grace hid in the Religious Education classroom during breaks because it was quiet, and the playground and attached sports field weren't.

Only one other, a boy with a brace and a sandwich box that smelled of cat food showed up now and then. Other than that, she had the run of RE's modest roost. It was, she thought looking back, ok. Not more than, but definitely, ok.

There had been teasing, of course – her old-fashioned name, her solitariness, her pastry-dough-coloured skin. Then being surrounded by adolescents meant being teased sooner or later for *something:* too tall, too thin, too fat, too flat, buck-toothed, birth-marked or just being quiet would do it – it wasn't hard to find a pretext. Being ginger-haired as well as pasty, thin and tall allowed no escape whatever. By seventeen, she was passing exams and deemed responsible enough to carry the attendance register from main building to school office every Friday. Which was how she came to the attention of the two lads in long trousers who spent their time hiding behind the science block smoking roll-ups. They catcalled and whistled. She ignored them. They tried every Friday for a month, each time a different name: just her, the two boys and the glassy indifference of the science block's filthy windows. It didn't feel dangerous, just embarrassing. *Cruella de Ville* and *Caspar the Friendly Ghost* were the only names she remembered. The rest, like the boys themselves, had been stupid enough to ignore.

The last time they crossed her path was as she walked through the park. And this last time was different. Maybe they were leaving, or maybe they already had, but this time the encounter was in the half-wooded stretch of grass that led away from the school towards home. An unlikely place, an unlikely surprise tactic. The first she knew they were there at all was when a stone, sharp-edged and fist-sized, sailed in from nowhere and punched into the breast-pocket of her blazer. It hit so hard, Grace stopped to catch her breath before she looked up. And there they were; watching. Grace straightened her back, raised her head and stared, as if recording their faces. Then for no reason she understood, she stretched a hand towards them, its fingers outstretched. Like a pantomime witch. The nearest stepped back, the other looking over his shoulder to check no one else was behind him. Using the moment, Grace took a single step forward and stretched as if to touch the nearest boy's face. Then she watched him double-take, and run. The other, finding himself alone with something stranger than he'd bargained for, followed. She watched them from her vantage point, clearing the trees and catcalling as they grew smaller. The words *fucking weirdo* rang out as they crossed open space to the railway station, then laughter. Laughter growing smaller. Laughter with an edge inside it, fading out.

What she had occasioned to happen and why, she had no real idea: the episode had something of the weird about it. But that didn't matter in the long run. Not if they kept their distance. Instinct in an emergency wasn't mental disorder, after all. Besides, it had worked. After a week without sight or sound of the pair, Grace allowed herself a brief moment of satisfaction that she had seen off trouble by doing nothing much. Just by being herself, whoever that was. By giving nothing away.

At the end of term, her mother went to her final parents' night and came back knowing some kind of altercation had happened in any case.

The janitor told me, she said. Two boys were hanging about after you and you said nothing. The janitor told me this, not you. He must think I'm a terrible mother.

I didn't tell him anything, Grace said, shocked by the janitor's awareness she even existed as much as anything else.

Then how does he know more about you than I do? Somebody must have told him.

I don't know, Grace said. I didn't tell anybody anything about anything.

So how does the janitor know these boys followed you?

Grace's eyes opened wide. You should have asked him that. I didn't need to *tell* anybody. It was a non-event. Nothing happened. They tried to scare me and it didn't work – that was all. I saw them off.

But they'd been pestering you for weeks. That's what he said. And you just let them. Why didn't you tell *me*?

Grace stood up, and they were suddenly too close. And Barbara noticed, for what was certainly the first time, how tall her daughter had become. Even in school flats. How separate. How sure.

I didn't tell you because there was no need. I looked after myself. You could try being pleased.

There was a silence, a shifting of gears.

I *am* pleased. If that's what happened. Then ok, I am.

Grace sighed.

Look, Barbara sighed. I get what you're saying. You told them to leave you alone or whatever and you say they did. I'm just trying to be sure you were all right. That they didn't – upset you. That's all. I just want to know you were fine.

Of course I'm fine, Grace said. I'm always fine.

Yes, her mother said. She sighed again. I'm only saying—

I know, Grace said. I know you're worried but there's no need. What I'm saying is I can look after myself. I've always looked after myself. You can let it go.

Grace watched her mother sit down on the sofa. She didn't, thank god, cry. But the talking was done. Embarrassed by the silence, Grace opened her school bag and shuffled the bits of paper inside, searching for home-work; something to disappear into. Her mother, catching the mood, leaned forward to switch on the tv.

The weather forecast stuttered into view, all signs and symbols. Warnings of scattered showers. The forecaster signed off and a parade of adverts moved into the screen space, a man in a tie offering a woman something he was sure was better washing powder than whatever rubbish she was using.

Can I put this off? Grace asked. You hate these adverts.

She did not bother to mention her own aversion to the damn things, mention that advertising for washing powder and chocolates, singled out for the attention of women, was vacuous to the point of inane and made her want to cry. Barbara leaned forward herself and turned the sound to nothing, leaving tie-man moving his mouth with no one listening.

Just one thing, she said. If you'd said something, anything at all. She paused, shook her head as if incredulous. I would have done something if you'd just said.

Grace didn't look up. Thanks, she said. But I'm fine now. They're gone.

Then she sat by the fireside, opened a page of calculus, and kept her head down. Her mother left the tv as it was and went out to the kitchen, the living room door open behind her. After a moment, the sound of the tap running into the kitchen sink told Grace her mother had moved on to something else. She turned to the symbols on the paper in front of her, then, having no interest in calculus, stared out of the living room window instead. Magpies in dinner jackets sat on the wall outside, a pair. Before long, she heard the radio filtering music down the hallway. It turned into the music she recognised, her mother singing in time with Paul McCartney. Hello, the same word over and over. Hello Hello.

Barbara chose to show up at the final school assembly and cried despite her promise not to. You didn't say you'd won a certificate, she said. Whoever made you clever, it wasn't me.

Grace knew more than to ask who else it could have

been. The identity of her father, the word *father* itself, was
not a question. Grace had never asked. It occurred for
the first time that day, watching her mother squirm, that
Barbara didn't necessarily know it herself. Asking now,
between the silent tv and mutual silent huffs was not the
moment either. The moment, she thought, waiting in line
the day she received her book token, the headmaster's
cursory handshake, would most likely never come. At the
end of the ceremony, such as it was, Grace was awarded
an extra prize: a modest allowance to get her off to a good
start at secretarial college. Exactly the kind of thing a bright
girl would wish to receive. The future on a plate. Barbara
cried again. She wasn't the only mum doing it, but was the
only single mum she knew about at the assembly room ceremony: beaming, weeping and ready for the Housewifery
Department's laden table of school-prepared tea and cherry
cake. It was that kind of day.

Less than two weeks later, Grace woke early and read a
few pages of her library book before bothering to get up.
Half-way downstairs in her nightie, she saw the bowl and
the box of cereal on the table, something that looked like
cards laid out for a game. Closer to was a can of peaches, the
tin-opener beside it. Only when she turned to the cooker to
switch on the kettle did she notice the plain, buff-coloured
rent book. It was open, with two five-pound notes lying
inside; beneath them, this month's payment date ringed in
blue. And beneath that, waiting in the subsequent month's
space, was the envelope. The address on the front was their

own, but scored out; the word *Grace* marked out on what little white space was left. She set the kettle down carefully and fetched the envelope to the table, and sat down. Slowly, as if there might be a trap inside, she opened the seal and found a single piece of paper, folded once, her mother's handwriting inside.

Dear Grace I have gone away. It may not be a surprise and if it is, I am sorry. I had not the heart or the way to tell you to your face. The thing is, you only get one shot at life. I raised you before anything else, and now you are so grown up, so clever. And now I have met someone, I want to grasp a new future while I can. There's a savings book in the bank till things sort out. It will make an allowance for you for a whole year. Be happy because life is short. I know you will be ok and I will always remember you. Be happy. mummy x

The words *savings book at the bank* were underlined. Grace read the whole note again, then let it fold back into its crease on the empty table space next to the waiting bowl. After a minute or so, she went back to the sink, poured herself a glass of water, and went upstairs. In her own room that still smelled of sleep, she pulled the curtains wide and opened the window, then got into bed and pulled the top sheet up against the chill. The sky showed through the open window space, the cloud outside shifting slowly. It blocked the light, then moved on by increments, dazzling her only when the edge of the sun grew fat again, claiming its space. Eventually, the cloud became a dull grey wash and the sky grew thicker. After a while came rain. As she settled back against the pillow, she heard the tap of what sounded like fingernails on the roof. Claws.

Pigeons maybe. Crows.

Map
First Aid/sunscreen
Batteries
Matches (waterproof box)

Shorthand, Typing and Basic Accounting promised to prepare her for anything, and in some ways, did. From two years' training to a six-month pool placement to a run of short-term contracts with fixed hours to a stint in a cramped office overlooking a brick wall, then a trio of not-entirely-wonderful contracts, she finally found the prize: Friedmann and Ricci in the middle of Edinburgh, solicitors and notaries. That the bus that stopped at their office left just across the road from her own place was, she decided, more than a lucky coincidence: it was a *sign*. From her first month, it was somewhere she felt she could settle if things worked out. They did. Even so, her time there was longer – better – than she'd experienced or imagined before. She was routinely informed, often thanked, left to her own devices. It felt the same as *trusted*. The Religious Education classroom but with a sense of purpose over and above escape, and a salary into the bargain. In exchange, she offered loyalty for the long haul.

Over twenty-six years with the firm – *the family*, as Mr Ricci called it – she never fell behind on a deadline or knowingly allowed a spelling error to survive. Her punctuation and grammar skills were, in the words of Mr Friedmann, *peerless*. Her tally of sick-days was seven. She lunched alone, enjoyed a joke, and famously told one herself the day Mr Ricci asked, in fun, if she knew any. *Why did the chicken go to the séance? To get to the other side.* It wasn't her only joke, but Mr Ricci had only asked for one. The rest were saved for another day.

More than once, Mr Friedmann asked if she'd like to have dinner with him if she was working late, and she'd point at the keyboard, raise an eyebrow and ask him to send a waiter round with coffee instead. And he did: coffee and a sandwich too, delivered by hand from the fancy place across the street. The offices at night were not a kingdom, but she had keys of her own and felt her work was valued.

It was new, this feeling of being valued by what were, in the end, strangers. Strangers with a firm of their own. Staying with people who valued her was not a difficult decision. Her colleagues were people she knew better than her next-door neighbours: that was more than likely the norm in this day and age. She knew who had children, who didn't, who was married, who divorced and who had a same-sex partner and no interest in making anything approaching a legal bond at all. And who had no boyfriend, girlfriend or anything between; the exception rather than the rule, the unremarkable singleton. Her, that's who. They knew she enjoyed listening to different kinds of music on the radio and fed someone's cat – she had no idea whose – when it turned up at her door on Fridays knowing there was fish. Little things, somethings and nothings, points of easy rapport. They did not know she loved museums because inside them she could be a schoolgirl again, examining the cases of heads, hearts and viscera in the Surgeon's Hall, chipped toys at the Museum of Childhood, paintings at the Gallery of Modern Art. She did not say she liked these places because they did not demand she be knowledgeable in advance or even ready to be impressed: only that she didn't steal or be noisy during the visit. Otherwise, she was free to make of it what she chose. She went to theatres, concert venues, cinemas; libraries, bookshops and market stalls and did much the same: almost everywhere in a city was a place to watch people, remark about the coffee or the weather or the shambles of contemporary politics if she felt like it and not if not.

Neither did she mention those places where a woman might have a drink alone or meet men with whom a single woman might converse and/or have sex without much of a fuss, but only at their house, calling a cab to go home immediately after. No exchange of addresses or numbers. Never. *Staying* over, even more as she grew older, held no attraction at all. However their lives worked, she imagined it was not like hers. They would not know how lucky she was in avoiding danger or misunderstandings, how much she relied on the goodwill of strangers, her own careful assessments. Younger men seemed to grasp the temporariness of these encounters from the start, but clarity, at least so far, had hurt no one. Or not for long. Edinburgh was rich in places to be fed and watered and entertained and in people who seldom asked personal questions. The ready esteem of the office, the reassurance she was not only proficient but very good indeed at her work and the recurring fear her mother might one day send a letter with photographs, made her appreciate privacy, separateness, little need to self-justify.

And on Sundays, if the sky was clear and not under the thumb of pollution, fog or heavy cloud, Grace could sit by the window and watch the stars to heavenly music or no music at all if she damn-well felt like it. It wasn't therapy. Just getting by. And the dreams kept coming, the return of once-frequent, now only occasional night-fears. The one in which she answered the door to find only a naked shop mannequin reaching to embrace her; another in which a letter arrived that, when opened, contained only the instruction 'do not miss me' that crumbled to powder between her hands when read, and on. And on. They came without warning or appeal, but being only dreams, meant nothing in the real world. Sooner or later, their pictures broke into pieces, retreated to their corners, and, after a fashion, passed.

*

In her final year with the firm (and how time flew if you were passing it in an even remotely palatable way) Grace went for the first time to New York, acting as personal secretary to Mr Friedmann. Four days, he said, to work in a different place with a different view out of a not-only-different but much higher window. Then again, if she had never been to New York, he imagined she'd find it at least intriguing. He wanted to take her, he explained, not just because she knew exactly his *modus operandi* and preferred requirements, because Grace, after all these years, knew what he was trying to say better than he did himself and having her by his side was more reassuring than he could say. Grace thought he probably could say if he tried, but she took the compliment as it was intended. Mr Friedmann, for all his prestige and his smart, expensive outfits, had never been a boor or thought himself a cut above. They were, so far as bosses and secretaries ever were, she supposed, friends.

And though Grace had never been anywhere so far away in her life – her holidays by and large had been one stripe or other of what was still by the skin of its teeth British – she enjoyed everything.

There was an unfussy room in an unfussy hotel, excellent coffee at breakfast and the towering windows over streets crammed with yellow cabs, people snaking through the spaces when they jammed at the lights. Folk moved faster here, allowing her to feel relaxed by comparison. Looking out of the twenty-seventh floor was like watching from a cloud. She had not expected to feel so much a watcher from a place apart, safe beyond danger, sudden shifts or blame behind this window in the sky.

On her final morning, a message arrived on her room phone. *New York is outside*, it said. *It's not raining. Meeting at 3 p.m. Try the Guggenheim.* The desk clerk smiled when she went downstairs, held out his hand. City map, he said. Mr Friedmann said you might need one. Have a nice day.

The Rockefeller Center's golden boy was first. Then St Thomas's Church, a cathedral cramped for space despite its size. Then a stroll and lunch in Central Park, leaving the rest for one thing. It showed along Fifth Avenue well before she reached it, part of the street yet somehow on its own. The Guggenheim was made in bright white slices, an unmissable space-ship of a building parked off-road for the afternoon. Inside, the stripes became layers of separate floors reaching in bandage strips from concourse to ceiling. She stood so long staring, the woman at the desk came over to ask if she was lost. Grace shook her head, eyes on a whirlpool of concrete.

People do get lost, the woman said. This is a big place. You can buy a guide for ten dollars, but if you're happy with surprises, go without.

Grace chose surprises: no names, no pack drill, no fore-shadowing of expectations. It allowed her to look without prior expectation or someone else's context: just the objects and canvases themselves. Those she liked best contained a story of some kind, more often than not a story that shifted depending on how long she allowed herself to look and take in detail. Paintings moved around inside. The content seemed to rearrange without warning, hidden objects or the place of things coming to light, slipping away. Her eye – maybe everyone's – absorbed things better when she took her time. When she singled out those that caught her attention, and stayed for a while.

In the next room she found, set apart from any other canvases and lit from all sides, a large, almost child-like painting filled with people, objects and buildings in a kind of dream-world: streets, houses and faces crowding together, yet each set apart. A window cast in blues and golds and reds took up one half, a glimpse of house showing fleetingly beneath, while outside, the town and sky filled with people, transport, living space. Close to, on the windowsill, a cat with a child's face was looking into the sky. In the right-hand corner, a head with two profiles looked forward and back from opposite sides while two stick figures in plain black clothing, a rabbi and his wife, lay sidelong on a cloudy road. Behind that, a pale city of high-rise blocks stretched out behind the Eiffel Tower, which glowed as it rose into the sky. The tiny man falling to earth from the top of the tower seemed in no distress at all; more like a child's toy, a paratrooper with a white chute or maybe the tip of the tower, falling.

The more she looked, the more crammed the canvas became. As if – she smiled to think it – the separate elements could shift, come to the fore- or background to suggest different ways of seeing; the painter only a go-between and the fragments with ideas all their own. The card gave no clues: *Marc Chagall, Paris through the window*. It was up to her to choose what it meant.

Caught up, she took a single pace back to see the whole thing at once, and bumped into someone else doing the same. A man, already apologising before she had as much as turned round. They spoke at the same time, then stopped, smiling awkwardly. She stretched out a hand to suggest a fresh start.

It's my first time here, she said. It's quite something.

He asked if this picture was a special favourite, and she told him not at all. It was the first time she'd seen anything like it. Coming to the museum had been a happy accident. She looked down. Sorry. I don't know enough to say anything clever. I just loved it at first sight.

Don't apologise, he said. You picked a good one. It's first time here for me too. At least first time *in the flesh*. I've always known this painting from books and postcards. But this is face-to-face. It's a big moment for me. He smiled. Like meeting Elvis.

Grace smiled, big and warm.

I don't know that much about painting, she said. It's new.

I was lucky there. An aunt sent me a postcard from New York because I thought I wanted to be an artist when I was fourteen. She said to go and see the real thing one day and – he shrugged – well. Finally I got round to it. This is it.

Not fourteen any more, Grace said.

Not by a long chalk, he said. I've taken my time. Did you come for any particular reason?

No, she said. Just curiosity. The one you're here to see is not like anything else. It just – caught me.

He looked at the painting again. It's something, he said. You can imagine him standing right there, making something remarkable from empty space. Trial and error, paint and repaint. Now he's gone and this painting is here, as full of life and colour and surprise as the day he finished it. It's something all right.

He shook his head, then blew his nose with a handkerchief. Sorry, he said. It's just – a bigger moment than I thought it might be.

Are you still an artist? she asked.

No. He smiled. I was only an artist in my head. In the real world, I was a civil engineer. I loved it. Then I didn't and I went into teaching. I remembered I loved watching people make things with paint, canvas, wood, clay, paper, anything they felt they could be at home with – the whole thing. You can live a whole life – work hard, be a useful citizen, make a good living. But the stuff that moves you, that you find by accident and know how lucky you are, given the odds, to have found it at all – that's the thing that makes sense of just keeping breathing.

Grace, moved by his being so open with a stranger, said nothing, let him look for some time. Then spoke quietly.

There's a café upstairs, she said. We could have a

restorative drink. She smiled. Would you like to sit with me?

Sure, he said. Yes I would. And I can buy us both a shot of caffeine at the least. He wiped his nose again, tucked the handkerchief away and raised not his right, but his left hand to shake.

Grace, she said, shaking in return.

Charles, he said. Charles Miller-Mendelssohn Douglas. But nobody calls me that. Everybody calls me Charlie.

Grace ended her afternoon with coffee and getting to know a little about a stranger. He had learned what he liked from books, he said, like most people do. Then he went to local galleries in Charlottesville, then in Virginia and now – now he had the free time to go to New York.

It's the stillness I like, he said. You look at a painting and your heartbeat slows and you sink inside a stranger's point of view. Even if they lived hundreds of years ago, you can still find something they made out of paint and sleight of hand and years of practice, something that survives because it's been stowed away and *it means something*. If it's special, it keeps meaning something. Like books. The more carefully you read – he opened his hands as if raising something to the light – well. You probably know this.

She did. Only when her watch alarm rang did Grace check the time. Time to get back. Time to get back right now.

I'm sorry, she said, standing up. I've really enjoyed this. But – I have a meeting. I just lost track of time.

He stood as she buttoned her coat. Tomorrow? he asked. I have one more day if—

I'm sorry, she said. I'm flying back tonight. I told you I wasn't much of a traveller: I only had a few days. This was my one shot at sightseeing, the rest was work.

Wow, Charlie said. I'm lucky to have met you at all. He rustled in a pocket as she closed her bag. Please, he said, take this? I had lots of them printed and almost never remember to pass them on. Today, I have. He handed her the card. In case you visit Virginia one day – get in touch. Please. We have fewer paintings than New York but lots more wilderness. Who knows? Think about it.

He didn't say *if you're ever in town* or *keep in touch*. Nothing awkward, nothing creepy. And Grace, knowing she was as likely to lose as keep hold of it, put his card in her pocket and ran for the stairs, the park, the start of rain. She attended her final meeting, typed the summary, then went to the airport with the case she'd packed the night before. Since Mr Friedmann was staying another day, she had the cab to herself, and two seats on the plane if she wanted. She didn't. No movie, no meal; all she wanted was sleep. Through her closed lids, the in-flight light beginning to fade, she heard the sound of the engine, the breath of too many people crammed in too little space. She hoped she'd dream about the painting, the face with two profiles. In the event, she dreamed of nothing at all.

Sunglasses
Knife
Water bottles/filter
Reflective blanket

Grace left the firm with no farewell speech and no one
pressed her to try. Less, she had always said, was more. She
didn't have a glass of wine from either of the bottles set aside
on the lobby desk, just a single shot of Mr Friedmann's best
malt. She embraced those who offered, thanked everyone
for the flowers then headed for the foyer to thank Alice at
reception and she was done. Brisk finish: bus-stop unclut-
tered, emotionally intact and almost clear-headed enough
to stay that way. It mattered very much not to cry, and
always had. It led to no good at all. Mr Ricci appeared at
a fifth-floor window as she looked up, raising his glass.
Grace boarded the bus and blew a kiss, not knowing
remotely why she had done it, waving from the upstairs
window as the driver moved off. That's what whisky in
the afternoon will do for you, she thought. Just one, my
god. She started to laugh, almost out loud. The bus was
warm and busy, full of tailings of conversation. Company.
Grace closed her eyes and breathed deep, opened them as
the bus turned a corner. Thank god she had never learned
to drive. She had the time now, of course. From today she
could do anything she damn-well liked. But first she would
spend some time working out what she damn-well liked
in the first place. The best part of work was feeling useful.

Being efficient and largely unobtrusive. Not to blame. The memory of a Christmas party some years ago, hearing one of the partners refer to her in conversation as *a genuine rock* to someone she couldn't recall came back. Alone at the back of the bus, she imagined a beach, cliffs made of sandstone, limestone, chalk. Something pale but more hard-wearing than it looked.

Six weeks later, the card fell out of her raincoat pocket. Charlie's card: a little the worse for wear, but legible, despite all the space his name took up. *Charles Miller-Mendelssohn Douglas, Charlottesville, VA*. His postal address, email and phone number showed white against a blue background on one side; the other held a quotation. *It's not what you look at that matters, it's what you see. Henry David Thoreau.* Looked up on her computer, Thoreau, whose name had rung only the faintest of bells, became a poet, philosopher, abolitionist, naturalist, tax resister, advocate of civil disobedience and lots more besides. They didn't come finer. That Charlie had picked this radiant individual made her smile and feel touched at the same time. First Chagall, then Thoreau: Charlie kept impressive company. Inspiring company. The same afternoon, she borrowed two books by Thoreau to find out what she had been missing, then went to the Gallery of Modern Art: a postcard called *Rabbi with Cat* by someone called Natalya Goncharova made the perfect choice. The rabbi and the cat in the painting they had shared were different, of course, but he'd notice the echo. It went that afternoon, reply address attached.

Thereafter came the correspondence: cards and email, the odd photograph of their respective front doors, garden birds, skylines. Charlie's house sat alone in a street of houses much the same. It had a sun-filled garden, a tiny lawn. Her flat was small and viewless and furnished with what her mother had left behind, but she sent a picture of her front door, the view from her window, the castle on a hill hardly any distance away at all. They did not, Grace noticed, send pictures of themselves. Charlie suggested video-messaging, but Grace wouldn't bite. Instead, he wrote an invitation in his best cursive and attached a small map of Charlottesville, showing its best face.

Dear Grace,

The white settlement in which I live is full of people who, like me, did not originally belong here. But we stayed and we have tried to behave better since. You can see for yourself should you visit. I have a second small bedroom for guaranteed comfort, or can offer a small tent in my small garden and a choice of restaurants across the street from the door or my own home-cooking. There are art galleries: we could visit at least one together if you would like that. And I would be very pleased to show you a little of my city, my state, and how life is lived here in the almost-South so near to the natural wonder of Shenandoah National Park.

I would love to welcome you. Visit Virginia. The Blue
Ridge Mountains will last forever, but I won't. Visit me.
Charlie.

It was something other people did every day, she told
herself. A short visit to someone's home. Things might
not turn out uncomfortably after all. And nothing was
irreversible. She wrote the words on paper to make them
settle in her mind: *Nothing is irreversible.* She had never
had anyone at her home to stay, never stayed at the home
of an acquaintance for even a short time. The thought she
might be imposing on someone's privacy or they on hers
had always seemed too close. At the same time, she was
refreshed by the exchange she and Charlie had had in New
York: from nowhere, genuine, warm and brief. Something,
however, made her uneasy about living in someone else's
home; a fear of being in the way, an error of judgement. But
there was time to think. To wonder if the risk of a visit was
being normal. For all she knew, it was.

Eight months after they began corresponding, in time to
catch the late-autumn leaves making their very best display,
Grace arrived at Richmond Virginia Airport, hoping she'd
be someone worth meeting on purpose instead of by accident. And there was the sign he said he'd promised to carry.
Welcome to America: tall blue letters on a white ground, high
over the heads of waiting families and taxi drivers, luggage
trails. *Welcome Grace.* She laughed, dropped the dead-weight
of her single case, and waved back, fingers spread in the

hope she'd be more visible that way. It had never occurred before how short she was by comparison to the local population: how nearly invisible in a crowd. But there was the big blue sign, coming closer step by step by step. Welcome to America, he roared: a great big voice, warm and clear, one hand, waving. Over the Atlantic! His face appeared as he came close, all his teeth – so many, so white – on show. I can't tell you how pleased I am you're here.

Grace took to Charlottesville. It was cheerful and light and the sky was huge. Charlie's house had a porch, a mailbox in the tiny space he called *the garden*, and a guest bedroom with its own bathroom and its own lock and key. His neighbours shook hands and welcomed her by name before she shook hands and told them herself. He drove her to Monticello and the Museum of Fine Arts and into the mountains where the leaves showed orange-red and deep for miles. So he didn't feel he had to take her everywhere, she took a cab for a couple of trips till it became a much more dull – even dulling – way to do things, then accepted Charlie's offer to revert to Plan A because not only could he act as tour-guide, it was more fun. Even more fun for him, in fact: nobody else ever wanted to hear his travelogue and his insights into flora and fauna. Just you, he said. If you want me to stop talking, you may have to shoot me.

After that, time together was *normal*. They took a trip to the mountains. They made fun of Fox News. They listened to the radio with their eyes closed. They kissed goodnight after a bottle of wine. And, without assumption, fuss or much surprise, eventually shared Charlie's bed, each wearing one part of Charlie's two-part pyjama set, talking till morning.

Her visa was a three-month thing, two months down and dwindling every day. Then, after only two days of thinking about it, Charlie stayed up in the junkroom he called *the study* with an ancient typewriter – his handwriting resembled a chimp's for godsake – and wrote out what he wanted to say.

Dear Grace,

It's been a while. Now I'm writing with a pressing question, and this way, gives you the chance to think it through. Here goes, clear as I can make it. Grace, Will you marry me?

This doesn't feel sudden, at least not to me. Don't confuse it with a desire for fuss, expense and caterers. Marrying is about two people. If we want, we can get the papers signed in days and wear the clothes we stand up in for the ceremony. The important thing for me is that we just do it. There are, of course, good reasons.

Every day, your visa expiry date, like sand in a timer, is running out. On the one hand, we could just let it, plan you come back after an interval, see how things go and not hope for the stars because – well – the bond I feel forming is maybe no more than a fling. But I don't believe that. In fact, I feel this is the perfect moment for us to come together with a commitment to the future in the shape of marriage vows. This process allows you to stay while we plan the future instead of accepting the enforced interruption/separation that would otherwise fall into place all too soon. You have to want this thing as much as I do. I present myself for approval.

I'm sixty-five. I've waited a long time. And here you are. We can act for ourselves and save time. Marry me, Grace. While I'm still here for the taking. I'm optimistic, solvent and almost good-looking. I love you heart and soul and I can't let you fly away without having said so.

Scraps and restarts, tying together a final copy, typing it out in full.

Done, he zipped the paper from the machine, signed and folded it then sealed it in a clean white envelope and wrote her name, almost legibly, on the front. It was two thirty in the morning. Charlie was about to send a letter to a woman already asleep in his own home. A woman who had crossed the Atlantic at her own expense to visit a stranger met by accident in an art gallery in a town neither of them knew. In its own small way, something remarkable. He walked down the hallway, breathed deep, and slid the envelope under the spare room door. She'd find it in the morning. That was soon enough. Mornings, in his experience, always came soon enough.

*

Charlie was nursing his second coffee in the kitchen when she finally appeared. Like Venus from the sea, he said, pale-skinned, her hair over one shoulder—

And wearing a dressing gown, she said.

My dressing gown, Charlie said.

She half-smiled, then looked down, fetched his letter out of a pocket to set on the counter between them. Ok, she said. Wearing *your* dressing gown. And trying not to look out of my depth.

Charlie waited, letting Grace pick her moment. She looked tentative. Unsettled. Maybe it wasn't surprising.

I don't know what to say, she said eventually. It's – it's a big idea.

I know, he said. It's ok to take your time. Within limits, that is. Otherwise you'll be heading for a plane before we've even talked about it.

She nodded, looked up. It's not about needing time, Charlie. It's me. I've lived alone for a long while. Neighbours, friends, people at work – sure. But after, I've needed a place to be alone. A place I could be sad or scared or whatever else I needed to be and be it by myself. She looked up, half-smiled. Keep myself to myself, just in case.

Charlie waited.

I've loved being here. I have genuinely loved being with you too. But I'm worried. I'm worried I would get scared. That I won't be the person you imagine I am right now, certainly not every day. That I might leave you a note one day and just run. I understand why someone would do that. Just run so you don't have to see how weak I really am.

Charlie hadn't been sure what his letter would do, but though this was unexpected, it didn't scare him. It didn't even surprise him. He had asked a big question, maybe not left enough room for her to think her own thoughts.

The thing with Grace was she *considered* things. She thought things through from one end to the other, took stuff seriously. Sometimes, now being a point in question, she was afraid she was not up to whatever *the task* might be. It had something to do with her mother's expectations of her as wiser than she felt. And, of course, the fact she had upped and run. Grace might be afraid a ghost of the experience would resurface, not in her mother this time, but in her own self. All those years of self-reliance, efficiency, then home to hide – he knew a little about that himself. But not the way Grace knew it.

I'm sorry, he said. I think maybe I've been too sudden or tactless or maybe even—

No, Charlie. She shook her head. You're never tactless. Clear, absolutely – but that's another thing entirely. You have no hidden side. It's me. I get scared. In case I'm not good enough, I suppose. Just in case.

Charlie put one hand gently on her shoulder. She was so small close to.

Maybe, he said. Or maybe you're afraid they'd let you down. Just disappear and not come back. I don't know.

She sighed, looked up at him.

He kissed her hair. And maybe there are other maybes. Like the possibility, just maybe, that your being here, in a place outside your own history and experience, with new people and new surrounds, might let you be someone else too. Maybe we could find a way to be spontaneous, even easy to be with each other. The way we have, in fact, managed to be with each other and everything else since you arrived.

Grace looked up. I hear you, she said. She kissed him, fetched his letter from the dressing gown pocket – *his* dressing gown pocket dear god she was still wearing his things – and held the letter he had written only the night before in one hand.

It's a great letter, she said. Have you written one of these before?

He smiled. He tilted his head back and laughed. No, he said.

Not at all?

Not at all. After a lifetime of making no marriage proposals whatsoever; of being *unlucky* and/or plain *lazy or avoidant* or whatever the hell, I wrote my very first one in the small hours of today. I'm new at this.

What pushed you? she asked.

I realised I was human after all. I wanted to keep finding out how you see things. Like the first time we met? The different things we saw in the Chagall painting? The different things you see *all the time*? You wake me up. You're another person entirely. The question is – and

I really thought you would ask me this today, I thought you'd ask this one right upfront – what would make someone like *you* want to be with no-surprises Charlie? Why would *you* take *me*?

Grace took her time. Eventually she spoke slowly. Well. You're kind. You have no vanity, no guile. You never panic. And you're always – *there.* You know how to be not too far, not too close. Just *there.* And that's a talent, Charlie. More remarkable than you seem to have any idea.

Less that two weeks later, they tied the knot in a local Italian restaurant with one officiant, one $30 licence, Rene, Georgette and Elsa (friends from Charlie's former lives) and a guy called Carlos playing *Mull of Kintyre* on the accordion while the whole restaurant cheered. Charlie was right: getting married didn't have to be a showcase and it didn't have to be expensive. All it had to be was truthful. And fun. It went, almost, without saying. Whatever else, it ought to be fun.

> Carry water.
> Do not drink water directly from streams.
> Follow trail blazes and use a map.
> Leave No Trace.
> Never walk around the top of a waterfall.
> Do not approach bears.

Grace remembered Elsa, even if their first meeting was

brief. It was two days after Grace first arrived, at a fund-raiser at Charlie's former school with lots of hand-shaking, a brief exchange about Elsa's grandchildren then going outside and how fresh it had seemed, Grace fetching drinks. At the wedding, Elsa's voice was familiar, the handshake too. She and Charlie had known each other forever, and she was glad he'd married: taking his time went to show how smart he was.

Some time later, Charlie invited Elsa to come for dinner. It was time, he said, for Elsa to reveal something about herself. Grace says we use cars too much here, he said. She misses walking. Maybe she'd like to take a walk with you one of these days.

Elsa laughed. That's easy, she said. Though it needs a little more planning than a walk in the park. Grace, how long have you got?

Elsa, her boys long grown up, was a trail walker and part-time volunteer at Shenandoah. The national park was a 105-mile run full of forests, waterfalls, rocks, trails and mountains, but words didn't say much: seeing it did.

It's true, Charlie said. It looks scary from a distance, but the route you choose makes all the difference in the world. People take children.

And mid-week means no crowds, Elsa said. Even at White Oak Canyon. Less than two hours each way with a walking stick, less without. We'd pick the gentlest conditions.

If I come, we'll have to, Charlie said.

Elsa smiled. What do you say? If you hate it, Grace, I'll eat my boots.

Elsa did all the planning. She pieced it together as a gift, and all Grace had to do was join in. That's how sure she was, how convinced it was true. All she had to do was find the will.

That first trip, to her own surprise as much as anyone else's, Grace didn't speak. Charlie and Elsa exchanged bits of conversation and Elsa rolled out names for rock formations now and then. But they were hushed most of the time, as if something might hear and run away. And though Grace had seen pictures – she was the homework kind – everything surprised her anyway; the sheer volume of a single falls as the water crashed down; the chill it scattered, the white foam. Most animals took care not to be seen at all, save the sole raccoon who appeared as they walked, stopping to stare back. Nothing was frightening, not even the couple who were sure they'd been trailed by a bear. Elsa's eyes said it all: they carried nothing to eat, after all, their bear-charisma lost at the first hurdle. Grace took no pictures, not even at Cedar Run where the rocks shifted into the wood of their own accord and they had to climb across – no height or distance, but requiring a degree of fleetness. Charlie crossed last. As they rose out of the woodland, the suddenness of the sky was close enough to touch. Why take pictures when you could watch? When a picture had little choice but to be a lesser thing?

In the end Grace walked the whole route, taking in the sound of their footfalls, the occasional scramble of claws as something ran to ground. Charlie remarked, in the middle of the final clearing, he had never seen her so – there was no other word – *radiant*. Sunlight, he said, something golden, shone from her skin.

Elsa wouldn't let anyone else drive back: this was her trip. And it worked out so well she could cry. The best of clear weather, the vistas, the unexpected lack of crowds or anything resembling them on the stretch they had chosen. After that, she sang along with the radio, focused on the road.

Grace sat upright, eyes wide open, Charlie asleep on her shoulder the whole way back home.

> Headbands
> Mosquito net/spray
> Cellphone?
> Journal

On the morning of her final birthday, Grace caught sight of herself in the bathroom mirror as she stepped out of the shower, hair streaming, skin pale as linen. She looked like a monochrome snap of herself at the age of four, small and naked on the sand, her mother almost in shot. Who had taken it she had no idea, but they had taken their time. The serious set of her stubborn little face, frowning as the sea rolled in; all white crests and glowering sky; herself on the sidelines, wearing an elasticated swim-suit and frown.

Maybe that had been a birthday too – the reason for the trip. Now here she was again, staring in the same way at her own reflection, looking for something she couldn't quite place. She shook her head, dried her arms. Charlie would be at college already, describing Chagall to whoever showed up; Elsa on her way, everything they could ever need on a camping trip in the boot. One year older never seemed likely, yet here she was. Time running through her fingers.

Elsa, five minutes early, had already placed Grace's bags inside the car. Over only three trips, they had developed a low-key packing strategy: two maps, one of their pre-ferred route and another with alternative sleep stops/ bad-weather shelters in case; one sleeping bag each, walk-ing boots and empty bottles to fill at trail towns as they went. If the weather changed, Charlie or Robert, Elsa's eldest boy, could drive a car over to their coordinates and take them to a cheap hotel, a warm bath, cooked food – treats against the outdoors taking a turn for the worse. Elsa had given up only once before, alone and without the children in tow. Only crazy people faced down tiredness and million-year-old rock formations with a bag of mixed nuts, a torch and a compass. It wasn't rocket science: you needed breaks and treats, reasons to march on. A hundred miles over twenty-four days gave time enough to slow down, take Sundays off and be lazy if they chose or sit tight if the weather set against them. Less than a month for a hundred unhurried miles, and the best time of year. Spring was always the best time of year. All that birdsong. Elsa couldn't wait.

The trees rose out of cloud-cover not long after first light. Elsa woke early every morning just to see it: you could sleep when you died, she said. Good weather and the wild to walk in were not to be denied. Moss and forest shades, grey-green-yellows and vegetable colours; fern and emerald and sea-blue pine. They counted crows, ravens and bluejays among quicker and less definable birds; the hawk, barely shifting high overhead was the best thing in the sky. Grace had almost taken along a guide book, a present from Charlie as yet underused, then changed her mind. You could look up in a book or look at a bird, a rock formation, a stream or a wild deer in the moments available for such things and the choice was easy, even if all it fixed in her memory was a glimpse of something with wings till it disappeared. Take your eyes away for a second and you missed something important. Shooting film or even camera shots were not a priority: keeping your eyes open was. They packed simple foodstuffs: oatmeal and coffee, cereal, biscuits, nuts, dried fruit, eggs and canned soup as standard, bottles to refill with water as they went along. Supply-stops were not hard to find.

Complaints – what bled, what hurt and what creaked or refused to bend on a downward slope – were passing references on the way simply to keep one's travelling companion informed, not a *bona-fide* subject of conversation. Describing an ailment soothed no one. Engaging with the surrounds – pointing out what caught the eye or sighting something unexpected, like the pair of wild turkeys who appeared and vanished in the same breath that second afternoon – was a real reason to head for the wild in the first place. Surprise kept heart and soul together in a trek. Unless, of course, it was the sort of surprise that made you run like hell. That had never happened so far, Elsa said. And Grace crossed her fingers and held her hands up to the sky for the rejoinder: *let's hope it stays that way.*

Talk they kept in general for evening, with luck sitting outside, smeared in sour-smelling lotion that kept black flies away, and watching the sun fade down.

So far, they had avoided snakes, biting ants and ticks. They were, and knew it, lucky. They had never been surrounded or staked out by raccoons, bobcats, skunks or bears, never seen a snake or an outraged owl drop from a tree: in general, the quieter you made yourself, the quieter the other beasts were too. Their preference, to keep completely to themselves as most animals, even the hungry ones did, was reliable enough. This place, Grace thought, rubbing her sore heels, her scratched ankle, the whiplash mark on her cheek from a rebounded tree sapling made her a contender for the most fortunate woman alive.

At the end of week three, the message was waiting at the

lodge when they came back from walking. Luray Police Department had called, reception said.

And this. The lady at the desk slipped a note over the counter. I'll bring you something in a glass so you can sit back and read it, she said. Then slipped out of sight.

LURAY 3678952: Robert Kane for Elsa Kane – urgent message: Come home, mom. Grandma admitted Greensboro (Moses Cone Memorial) C'ville drive time just over one hour. Let me know how to find you or send TOA if you are OK to drive, but come. Will call once in range. Love, Rob.

ps Jane and kids are in Greensboro. I will wait here to be with you.

Elsa read it again and closed her eyes. Gently, Grace took the note from her and read it herself.

Elsa. I'm so sorry.

Elsa said nothing.

You should go back. He'll wait for you. Go back.

Nothing.

You could send a message – they'll have a line here. Either way, you have to go back.

They had made no contingency for emergency: the compass, the two-way radio, everything else assumed no rethink, no Plan B.

We have one more night here right here, Grace said. I

can make cancellations or whatever tomorrow. Right now I think I should book a SwiftCab and hope they come before too long. Or we could get a lift to the entrance park, find you a cab from there then come back and dismantle the site. Unless you want Rob to collect you in the middle. He has a car, right? The route to Skyline Drive isn't difficult. What do you say, Elsa? What do you—

Elsa held up one hand like a traffic cop. I say let's think slowly, she said. I just need to think. She closed her eyes again, breathed deep and put some pieces together.

You should stay here, ok? Deal with the bill tomorrow and pack up and everything that goes with it and that's a load off on its own. And if you can do that part, there's nothing to stop me going back tonight. It's not a hard decision. Fetch us those drinks, and I'll make some kind of plan.

Grace did as she was told. One gin, one whisky and some tap-water were waiting for her, already laid out on a tray. By the time she arrived back at the table, Elsa was businesslike.

Ok, she said, chiming her gin with one hand. Short and sweet. I want to head straight for the hospital – that's not in question. Then I can speak to hospital staff and I can do that on my own. Rob isn't the hospital type. Not even when he was born there. I want to hear what the doctors have to say first-hand and not half-way down the interstate on my sons's phone, so that's exactly my plan. But you, she looked up, met Grace eye to eye. I think you should stay on.

Grace said nothing.

You're experienced now, and this trip has been well planned. The route, provisions, plans, even the medical kit are all in place. I know how much this birthday trip means to you, how much you've looked forward. I'll tell Charlie you're making up your mind, and how you'll make the best decision. He knows already, but it won't hurt to know it twice. He might want to fetch you back himself when you're done. She squeezed Grace's hand. And either way, we'll both be fine. Every last one of us, Grace, will be *just fine*.

Grace listened in silence, sipped her drink. Elsa was a natural organiser, flush with single-mom skills. She did it so well you didn't notice it opening out, setting things in order till it had. Elsa three jumps ahead of everyone else. Her idea was perfectly sound, even liberating. It was also scary at the same time.

Ok, Elsa said. You think. I have to pack. The rest I'll plan on the way.

As she turned, the receptionist stood behind them, ready to speak.

I didn't mean to pry, she said. But I understand one of you is headed to Charlottesville tonight. Or not far off there? She picked up the empty glasses. It happens my daughter is headed that way herself and will be very happy to take whichever of you it might be, if that helps. If the destination isn't too far off her planned route, she'd be happy to accommodate. Her name is Carolyn, she's thirty years

old and she's a driving instructor. The woman smiled. Safe
hands. May I tell her you'd like some help? Or have you
already made other plans?

The tension in Elsa's shoulders smoothed out. Grace
watched her melt, like ice in the sun. That would be wonderful, thank you, she said. Her voice was small again,
relieved. I'd be very pleased indeed. Thank you. Thank
you both.

She almost cried.

Elsa packed while Grace thought, the idea of staying still
turning in her head. She already had everything to hand:
the contact phone, the emergency kit, the first-aid pack. All
the tracking, planning and heading in the right direction
stuff. Having no one to verify her map-reading worried her
a little more, but using the compass was simple enough.
All the decisions had been made on the nights of planning. This far had taken several days, everything noted
in Elsa's tidy handwriting. Every decision had been made.
Travelling on alone, however, was not something she had
ever considered.

Elsa, done with packing, offered up her camera.

It's idiot-proof, she said. I know you're not the kind who
has to take pictures, but just in case. She clicked the *on*
button, snapped, showed her result. See?

Grace saw a picture of her own face, the corner of the tent
behind her. Everything crystal. The camera, when she took
it in her hand, weighed nothing at all.

Up to you. Elsa checked Grace's indecision, and hesitated. Am I bull-dozing? You know that taking-over thing I do, making wrong assumptions? She sighed. I'm just – wound up. I don't mean to boss you into a corner, just after all the planning and the looking forward—

Stop, Grace said. You're not assuming or bossing. You're making sure I know the options and it's ok. And I do. I'm thinking it over, taking my time. Things are shifting around is all. I'm not sure.

OK, Elsa nodded. If you're still not sure by tomorrow—

Then Grace interrupted. If I'm not sure by tomorrow, she said, I'll wait till I am. I'll ask advice. Trust I'll be fine. Who you need to look after right now isn't me.

A car horn sounded outside, insistent in the still air.

I'll bring you pictures either way, Grace said. Now go.

Carolyn sat in the driver seat of a dusty four-by-four. You're taking my friend to Charlottesville, Grace said. They shook.

Ready when she is, Carolyn said. Her son is taking over for the Greensboro stretch – we'll work that out on the way.

Elsa arrived at the passenger door, dropped her bag inside then turned to Grace with her arms wide. Grace embraced back, then watched Elsa slide inside the car, Carolyn smiling from behind the wheel. Carolyn had strong white teeth, a tattoo of Jesus making a thumbs-up on her arm.

You take care, she said as she turned the ignition. And so will I.

Grace watched the truck wheel out of the park, listened as the sound of the engine grew distant. Overhead, the sky was closing. No rain. No cloud-cover. Just dark, moving in. Tomorrow, she'd decide what she decided.

She was sixty-six years old. Old enough to know their months of preparation meant something. Old enough not to allow fear a place. The small cache of diazepam, the last-minute thought, her *just-in-case,* would settle her thinking if she was still confused tomorrow.

That first night alone, the forest was noisier outside, but that was a trick of the ear, the mere fact of one inside a space for two. Now and then, she heard small things snuffling in the dark and wondered what they were looking for, what kind of beasts they might be. The important thing was knowing that they were, they were not looking for a human being. It lived in the vicinity, that was all. The scrambling of claws that startled her from sleep in the small hours happened only once: a possum more than likely, rooting for cookies, oatmeal, chocolate or any other damn thing to grab with those little human hands. She turned in her sleep, listening till it scuttled away. And the next she knew it was morning.

    Insect repellent
    Whistle

Binoculars

Tarp

She watched the sun as she drank her coffee, checked the blue-penned route on the map, then dismantled the tent. She washed the cup, gathered up the trash and checked she had left everything as she had found it. Then looked at the sky.

From the first step, the route is your companion, not your adversary.

That was what the guide said, its very first sentence.

She took the pack on her back, the tent in its thin cover rolled up beside it.

You're only young once, she said out loud, watching the sun make a line on the horizon. Decision made. Who knew? She might even walk all day.

Alone wasn't as alone as it sounded. Not when you got down to it. Sleep came easier at night from the first – the opposite of what she had assumed – at least to begin with. When handling the map became awkward outdoors, she made sketch maps instead, noting directions and significant markers on the way. And she thought about Elsa, making sure she did things by the book though no one was watching her at all. One old signpost marked the way to a cemetery, a reminder of a time when people had lived here, built homes and raised families before moving on, leaving only these faint traces. Mostly, only the cemeteries remained. She turned away from the temptation to follow, kept strictly to the marked route. Safe. People said hello if they crossed on the same stretches, made conversation. Most of the time, she was, quite happily, alone.

By day three, she reached the expected dip in the road that widened out into flatlands, clusters of wildflowers stretching as far as the eye could see. There would be a spring and a waterfall before long where she could refill the flasks, take a break in the sunshine. After that, all this greenery would give way to bush, thicket and the climb to a promised mountain view. The route was plain as day, clearly marked in red with arrows, exclamation points and circles for emphasis. Foolproof. If the weather was willing, she'd reach the half-supply point soon. Half-way. One more day at most, if the weather held good. It showed every sign it might. One day.

The morning of the fourth day, Grace woke past sunrise, the air inside the tent thick. The dip marked on the map had shown *en route* as expected, but had not led to flatland as the note suggested. It led to scrub, then a dry patch of nothing much at all. One mile further on, grassland showed up, but no sign of collectable water. Worried, Grace found her sunglasses and looked over the stretch ahead. Not so much track as a scrappy pathway, meal-worm brown earth and bark chips, dry as chicken feed. Blinking, she counted the sawn-off stumps, the spindly birches clustered in the distance, so high their tips came together to make cracked glass of the sky beyond. The other side showed only a thinning track and hump of sand and bark chips worth avoiding. An ant-hill more than likely. An ant-hill for sure. Probably teeming. The vague doubts that had crept up on her from time to time and that she had dutifully pushed away, pushed away, pushed back. This time hard. This wasn't the right road.

She had taken a premature turn, or just a wrong one, and come to a place that was not where she should be.

She breathed out, slung the tent down and unrolled the pieces, managing worry. Putting up the shelter she had down to an hour. Blankets, flashlight, night light, two cans of water and trailbars, still in easy supply, would do for now, the rest of the supplies, such as they were, she strung up for safety in the trees out of reach of snakes, raccoons, anything likely to sniff out food and climb.

At some point during the night, she woke, hauled the trail map out of her neck-chain carry-case, and opened it out like a carpet. After that, she slept, fully clothed, the tent door zipped and locked.

Two trailbars, a half-bottle of cold tea and a shot of whisky helped in the morning. Taking it slow.

Nothing looked any more as it should outside, but low sun filtered through on the clearing floor, bright gold tri-angles through the leaf cover. This day was for map-study till the map began to mean something once more. Off-track happened now and then: a way back would come clear.

Drawing thin pencil lines from where she had started, she tried to see something that looked like where she was now. Something leading down instead of up. The map resisted for hours, refusing to make sense. Eventually, she went outside the tent for better shelter, to find a landmark, a marker with an arrow, even a single word cut into wood to suggest a place name or direction. In more than an hour of walking deeper into the forest, she found nothing: no new viewpoint, nothing that suggested people at all. She went back to where she started and tried the opposite track, only to find it petering into dry scrub, leaves and reddish earth, willowing into a snake-thin strip. To search deeper meant taking the tent and equipment: the risk of leaving it here was crazy. So she walked back, eyes open. Something, anything, would eventually show.

Back inside, her mouth dry and stomach tight, she drank down most of what remained in her flask and counted two stay-cool bottles left. She'd have to walk further, listen for the sound of water to suggest a marker. But right now, all she wanted to do was check the most useful thing she'd packed was still there, still ok. Under her toothbrush, nail scissors, eye drops, sting-relief and tiny packets of god-knew what else, they eventually showed, tightly bound so nothing could find and take them away; two blister cards of twelve pills each, yellow- and green-coated little cluster-bombs for times of trouble, for in case, in case, in case. And since that *in case* was already here, she unwrapped the tissues, popped three capsules from the coating, washed them down with the warm dregs she had saved from yesterday and looked at her watch.

It was four in the afternoon and she was scared. All she had to do right now was wait till the diazepam allowed space to think in a straight line again. God bless diazepam in all its forms. Her eyes watered. Three a day for as long as they lasted. Three a day. Then she'd have to keep going another way. To help, she lay down, arms by her sides, and forced her breathing to slow. She imagined a clear mind. A stretch of road, growing wider with each step, rolling back the way she had come.

It was still dark when she gathered wood by torchlight. There were crows. Almost laughing. The sound they made was not, as people said, harsh. It was curious. Taking stock. She wondered if they knew she was unsure, what they would make of it. Then, sobered up, she went on gathering. Wood scraps would make a fire that anyone coming into the wooded space or flying overhead would see. She should search for a stream too, but making the wrong decisions risked heading further in the wrong direction. Even if she took the tent, that was too big a risk. Instead she found a space where the orange fabric might show through, catch the eye of anyone walking nearby, someone with binoculars maybe. There were lots of birds here, mostly invisible but their calls never far away. She moved everything a short walk away, one piece at a time, reset camp, and found the compass. In her sleeping bag's secret pocket, well concealed. Elsa must have put it there, stowed safely, never too far away.

Grace opened the box. There were no instructions inside, no paper at all, only the clearly marked dial, the living magnetic track. At least she had plenty of time to experiment. The only thing she knew for sure was that pointing the red needle tip on N and aligning it in turn with the map showed true north. That was it: a phrase Elsa had taught her as they headed out in the car what seemed like a long time ago on her birthday; nothing more. But something. If she worked out where she was, or where anything else on the skyline was, the way back might suggest itself. She had plenty of time to try.

Outside, unsure on her feet, she held the cup in her right hand and watched the needle flutter. If she moved suddenly, it wheeled. Shaken, it scudded then trembled in whatever direction she turned the case. Every time, only stillness and the right alignment married the red tip with N. Every time. Heart trembling, she walked slowly to a spot where the ground spilled steeply behind the trees, ceding to a drop where the shale had cracked open. Kneeling back from the lip, surrounded by fresh, clean air that seemed to belong with the ritual, she opened her hand and held up the silver circle. The needle quivered, then wheeled. She had not held her hand still enough. It had to be still. She closed her hand over the glass face, opened it, then held it out again, waiting for the needle not to tremble. Then the same mistake. The slightest movement, it seemed, broke the spell. After one more try, wondering if the needle arm was out of practice, she shook the case to help it free. Softly at first. Then again. And felt nothingness as it left her hand and became a sound instead, the thin sound of metal and dull rubber, bouncing. Nothing showed as she looked down, only the thin crack of rock, the sound of something falling. Bouncing. Again.

Again.

Again.

Again.

That night was long. It was very dark indeed. No more nights outside the tent. It was stupid. She filled the tent with ant spray, a sharp, synthetic smell that made her queasy, and made herself stay inside. Walking would find something edible sooner or later, but water was another matter. The last bottle was done, the empty plastic shell taken by godknew what in the night. She had heard nothing, seen nothing, which meant the diazepam was finding its mark, at least. Now, however, the need to find water mattered more, pushing her to walk every day, heading when possible to higher ground. She keyed texts into her phone on what little charge remained, but they only stacked up under the NO SIGNAL sign and the screen, its eye closing, went dark. All she could find on the radio, the battery of which seemed to be lasting forever, were what sounded like or might even have been echoes of distant space. White noise, arguing with itself. Nothing like human voices. Nothing like a single human word.

That night, the torch battery blinked, dimmed then went out as she wrote a note for Charlie. For a long moment, it felt like the whole world had disappeared. But reaching with her fingers, pressing against her skin, proved her eyes were still open. Not even a moon outside. There was nothing to see. Bats twittered like telephone wires outside as she drew the mylar sheet closer. Warm. Almost.

Next morning, her hands, when she woke, showed the first trace of gold.

For two days, the gag reflex and her tongue unsticking was the unseemly start to the day. Outside, at least one crow, creaking. Spilling her notebook aside as she tried to sit, she looked down at her hands; how faded her nails had become, how clear the bones beneath the skin when she flexed the joints. Skin bright as sunshine all over again. There was no more pain, no urge for food, even drink. Just birdsong which made her weep. The scent of something sweet and heady, hung with pollen, filled the tent and she rose to meet it. Her eyelids felt thin, almost jagged. Like the edges of paper. Very thin glass.

That she should write a note was obvious. The thought melted and recurred, less pressing every time. She wanted Charlie to know she had thought of him, that he had changed her life and she was grateful, that she was lucid. All she had to do was open a fresh page, write something down before she forgot. He would want to know what she had seen, what she knew for sure. One careful letter at a time.

Every morning now for close on five days, the sun comes to meet me. It filters through the roof vent in a single shaft of light. And turns my hands to gold.

Blue rope, tumbling from the corner of the orange tent.

If she had fallen asleep, she woke not feeling tired any more. Just awake. Alert. She lifted her hands and stretched her fingers wide. They were, as expected, changed. The blanket fell as she stood, steadied, framed her hands against her back to support herself to full height.

Elsa would be back home. Charlie would be in that tiny patch he called a garden, maybe, planting something to show her when she came back. She stood after a fashion, reached out to the tent frame where the sun came through, and slowly, carefully, unzipped the door.

There in the sky directly above her head was what looked like an angel. Gold, with a face not unlike her mother's but softer, less tired, looking out over the gold and green landscape, the black underside of the long avenue of trees. As if more had grown in the night, meshed together like a shield against blinding her. The figure in the sky trembled, its wings becoming still. Till slowly, piece by piece, it began to resemble an eagle, larger and more beautiful, its eye upon her the longer she stared. The cloud thickened, turning brighter as the bird-woman's feet unfolded, slowly, cleanly, like grappling hooks on farm machinery. A voice, maybe Charlie's, spoke in her head. *Why would you take me, Grace? Why me?* And the bird came closer, a picture of everything beautiful. As if it might recognise her at last.

It could carry a whole deer in those claws.

Carry it clean away.

burning love

I made a pyre.

That ugly bloody sofa I habitually hid bottles behind because she thought I drank too much, the curtains from the bedroom her hand had touched, the sheets her body had moved against and which stubbornly still smelled of her, the lamps with shades trailing from their necks that she had taken the bulbs from before she left. I took boxes of cereal from the kitchen, the sugar cubes she used to put in her Coke (*I don't like fizz*), the Cherry Blossom and Brasso tins, plastic-bound scourers she insisted were part of her battery of normalcy in someone else's house. I swithered about the Ajax and the dusters because I used them too, but went for them in the end. This stuff would burn. It would plume up easy, given the right incentive and I already had that – the cleaning substances, made for arson, bottled inferno. I peeled strips of paper from the living room and hauled cushions out by the ears, rolled the rug she liked so much into a fat cigar in the hope it would smoke. I turned out boxes of biscuits, old photographs, flaky piles of envelopes and occasional letters, bills, flyers, those withered yellow sheaves of the obituaries she had clipped and collected for years, the cardigan I bought her that she did not wear because she never liked it anyway.

Then it dawned: what I really wanted was books. Her books. I could see them, smiling down at me like tattooed dentures from the shelves in the shed she kept as a work room. If she thought I'd forgotten about the shed, she had another think coming. I'd poke her fucking shed-sheltered library with a poker and burn it to funerary ash. It crossed my mind she might have taken the key, but no: the Sunday hats, the faux-fox stole she wore to stave off the cold hanging like a blood-sucked bear on a single hook were in there, all together, with a tartan rug. Royal Stewart, the tartan of punks and Pretenders. In need of something to keep me going at this pitch, I fetched my phone and the portable speakers I paid a fortune for that made everything sound like Wagner, and turned the music up full bung. John Shirley-Quirk to start with. I had to be pumped with melancholia, roaring with animal pain, and this voice delivered it in spades. That done, I set about selecting books.

Sylvia Plath first, the Boston Harpie and her bastard daddy together in the one coffin, a slim volume with a blue spine. *Love set you going like a fat gold watch* – indeed, indeed. Ted Hughes next, then Rilke, MacCaig, Neruda and Carol Anne Bloody Laureate Duffy – *I'll give you an onion* all right, you eye-watering bitch. I raked further back for what the damp had already kissed, found the musty copy of the *Complete Sonnets*, the black-bound Shaw with the gold lettering flaking onto my fingertips, the bloody John Donne. There were some sixpenny Woolworth numbers, things about vampires and supernatural intelligence reaching pre-monotheist civilisations, aliens from hostile lesbian planets, new society rubbish and *How to Change Your Man* cobblers she had rightly hidden from me all along: a David Icke book about the Queen Mother being a lizard, a splay of dried-up Margaret Atwoods (*The Bloody Handmaid's Tale* on top), a Doris Lessing doorstop with the author looking like she disapproved of everyone who would never learn the lessons of the fucking veldt and Barbara Gowdy's *We So Seldom Look on Love* that had made me weep till I filled my ears with salt, imagining the betrayal that would one day certainly come. As it had, it had. Record sleeves, kept for the lyrics on the back, summed Bowie, Eminem, Hugo Wolf and Big Bill Broonzy. I kept the Bowie. The rest went outside. I tried to throw the whole lot up with my arms – something I'd seen in a film – but of course it was too heavy. Instead of lifting and falling in slow motion, it spilled with a damp thud on all the rest already in place on the grass as the twilight cramped down. I caught my breath. The sorting and rejecting were over. It was time to construct.

In a nest of paper twists I strangled with my own hands, I set the king-size firelighters, rags soaked in kerosene and the box of all the hair I'd saved over the years from hair-dressers' floors. Everything else I booted on top – from the books to the cleaning fluids to the soiled, spoiled food-stuffs – then booted it again to make the shape just right (there's always a let-down if a pyre is not triangular). Done, I fetched the fancy speakers and my phone from the shed and the 1812 overture found its feet at one touch of the remote control. As the music lowered its horns for the full attack, I cast the petrol drained only this morning from our once-shared Mini Cooper over the whole bloody lot. This useless gamut of art and sound and words and stuff that had meant her, that had once meant so much to me, and that I had put here to make sure it never meant any such thing again. No more running in circles: this finale would be inexorable. It would solder every broken fibre in my macerated heart till it reached the very core and cracked it clean in two. I did not need to wait.

From a single match held close, the flames took quickly. And all I had to do was let them. Surplus to requirements, able only to surrender, I moved closer, closer. Closer till my skin felt it would blister. Until, in fact, it did. It would reach her hair, the love letters around which it was woven, then the kerosene. It would find me soon enough.

fittest

The weather had been weird for ages, but this summer was wild. Warm, heavy rain every morning shifted to high winds, howling winds and tree-shaking bluster by noon. Long humid evenings, the sun emerging fitfully like a jaundiced eye between bruisy clouds, brought an end to more days than most cared to remember. There was even a freak shower of giant hail, ice-balls hard enough to shatter as they landed, spilling seeds, or maybe insect eggs, over the pavements of Braemar. Not to be outdone, Stornoway reported fleets of basking sharks ramming boats offshore. Perth had a shower, a genuine downpour, of live eels. The Central Belt was milder by comparison, but no one would have called it pleasant. Save for the occasional olive-tinted tuft, grass showed only in shades of straw and brown. When an intercepted film shot by Grampian police surfaced on YouTube suggesting the sky near Inverness was turning bronze, those of us who paid attention to our instincts began, like salmon, drifting north.

Despite warnings of likely petrol shortage, I took the

caravan. Old engines don't let you down and this way I could ferry the bike on the roof, just in case. The cat wouldn't come – she's not a traveller at the best of times – so I left the flap unlocked and plenty of food, set the tap to a dribble and left her to it, telling myself she'd be fine. Beasts, unless you deliberately crippled their chances, usually were. Nonetheless, guilt and worry nipped at me as I drove over the hills. No deer. No Highland cows. Nothing looked right.

Despite the driechness of the drive, I was there before I realised, the loch showing suddenly over the gorse like labradorite under heavy cloud. A wispy ectoplasm floated above the water's surface preparing to evaporate the moment the sun broke through, only the sun wasn't for breaking. The water itself was as still as ever, but swollen. Horribly swollen: near convex, like a cow in calf.

Taking nothing for granted, I parked behind a clump of spruce trees and scrambled up the nearest crag, scanning the surrounds for – what? Clues, maybe? A landmark that said I was somewhere else entirely? Most likely, something as weak-willed as company. And there they were. Spread like sheep on the downside of the verge, their tents and their transport, their animals and children, washing lines like flags in the wind. A whole camp, it seemed, had arrived before me, massed, however loosely, for what was most likely the same reason I had begun this journey myself. The tweed set, having sought out less sodden clumps of moss, perched on shooting sticks near the edges of the lake, keen to observe what they took to be their terrain more closely.

Others had gathered driftwood and stood chatting or simply staring near smoky fires. Behind them, fishermen cast lines. I glanced over my shoulder to the caravan, hoped it was camouflage enough, and tipped my boots over the downward slope to join them.

Next day, I left the caravan shortly after dawn and approached the encampment by a devious route, fearful of giving away my home. Either I had miscalculated, or the number of settlers had doubled overnight. Two saddled ponies fed from open sacks at the waterside and a handful of chickens, with no coop in sight, scratched at nothing under a barren tree. A man in a cloth cap had set up a deck-chair and held a flask as he smiled absently over the water. There were tents, teepees, a makeshift lean-to and open-backed vans, and further off, a painted contraption not unlike a dog-sled, its tangle of harnesses empty. A couple of boys in biker boots played heavy metal hits to the queue at the snack van offering all-day breakfast rolls with black pudding or sausage. I ate from my own provisions out of preference, watching monster-hunters, nut jobs who had come in hope of a brief glimpse of Nessie from the vantage point of higher ground. A girl in tiger face-paint had set up a stall with helium-filled balloons and inflatable hammers and an ice-cream van came round the brae with a jangly outburst of *Greensleeves*, the strains of which made a trio of divers break the surface of the loch like seals. People took photographs. Why not? There was charm here, an air of festival. Even I could feel it.

At night, my natural caution restored, I saved the torch and washed my socks in the dark, taking my books to bed unread merely to keep them dry. I needed them for reference, after all, these maps, tables of edible flora and, if it came to it, fauna, and some were old, already out of print. I could not risk loss. Irredeemable loss.

Next day, the god-almighty whirr of helicopter blades brought a fly-over of military sorts and freelance hacks with long-lens cameras. I assumed they were scanning the loch, but it might have been the crowd: the hippies and hoboes, students and amateur geologists, tourists, the rubberneckers and the trainspotters that made up our group. We were radio hams and lone rangers and people with no real home to go to, it was true, but we were also families. People had brought their kids. Silent, in the main, the folk with kids, especially if they were teenagers, exuded an aura of mild trepidation and not much nonsense. Some of their kids looked bored shitless; others, plugged behind earphones, kept themselves to themselves, radiating the words I AM NOT WITH THESE PEOPLE. But they were. Some things teenagers still must learn the hard way.

I wasn't the family type. Not for a second. I thought that, my mother said, then I realised the clock was ticking. You'll change your mind. Wait and see. But I wouldn't. She had no idea how much she rubbed me up the wrong way without even meaning to. It was a general problem with human beings: very few of them read signals, signs, the set of another person's face. They were, by and large, all right Jack. The world didn't need more people, it needed less people. Whole species were dying because we were using up all the space, all the food, all the everything. The group I identified with here, if any, were the loners, people who, I noticed, were the thoughtful carriers of effective supplies: books, compasses, axes, wire and rope, picks and fish-hooks, knives. We had thought about the same thing. I could tell my kind at a glance: irrespective of gender, we wore trousers and we carried knives. We carried lots of knives.

That same afternoon, the rain came back so hard it hurt. Some people moved out, or tried to, but their wheels rutted, spraying loam. As the sky darkened, faces that had begun to be familiar slid monkishly under the hoods of their jackets, and those without hoods wore supermarket bags, skin streaking with water as they ran. The priests – so similar they might have been twins – shut their innovative travelling confessional and shifted to drier land just before the deck-chair, the refuge of the elderly man I had not seen for a day now I thought of it, disappeared under a slick of loch-side mud. In disarray, the encampment shifted to higher ground, clanking and clustering like Roman soldiers resettling their shields against the Persians. *When the sky lifted, they said, tomorrow; when the ground was less treacherous.* For now, we could only wait. Numbers meant safety. We bided our time.

That night, I burned the torch for hours, checking routes, gambling they'd be unsubmerged. I whittled sticks, ignoring the whine of a dog outside that seemed lost or abject. I must have slept eventually, because something woke me. Through the low burr of morning rain, a beating noise. A slow, thick pulse. Awake immediately, I hauled on my boots and went outside.

In our sodden clothes, from the lip of the ridge, we – for there were many of us alert now – looked down at a loch that even from here was visibly bloating further. The rains, of course, but something more was at work. Perhaps a rift had formed at an unthinkable depth between the loch, the River Ness and the Caledonian Canal. Could it be that the darkest basins beneath Loch Ness had finally opened and the long-denied sea was rushing into the freshwater vacuum? Maybe this, in turn, had led to the death agonies of freshwater fish and deep-sea invertebrates which showed on the surface as this tormented, implacable bubbling? Someone cranked up the volume of a radio, fast-forwarding through every channel in quick succession for news. We heard zip-fast fragments of jazz, a female voice intoning that all roads in and out of Westminster were blocked, a flash of Connie Francis singing *Who's Sorry Now* and Radio nan Gàidheal warning tourists not to go out without a rain hood in English and Gaelic. An umbrella, the presenter joked, would just help you blow away quicker. *Leave the bugger in the hall stand!* Radio 1 fronted an astrologer who insisted the Loch Ness monster would make an appearance that very afternoon; either that, or there would be extraterrestrial communication. Interference carried off the invited response of the Archbishop of Canterbury before Radio 2 screamed out the opening bars of the *Dr Who* theme. With a cry of frustration, the owner of the ungovernable radio had no alternative but to cut the sound. Then there was only silence.

Thick, almost dark silence.

In the unaccustomed calm, the earth was steaming gently, allowing excess water to evaporate as the sun rose. The rain had stopped.

The rain.

Had.

Stopped.

The priests were the first to rally, setting up votives under tarpaulin and handing out free cigarettes. There was laughter, a general softening of shoulders and shaking of hands. Tyres were checked with a view to moving on when the mist cleared, fresh tea gratefully sipped in proper cups. An elderly woman began to practise t'ai chi. It was then I noticed what made the human sounds, small as they were, so stark. There was no birdsong. No cries of crows or sparrows, not even a gull. I had a fag while they lasted and snapped my maps into the pockets of my cargoes. Two books, a knife and a slim-handled pick. A phone card. In case.

The dry spell continued just long enough to begin to seem normal. Then the earth, done with resting, girded its loins.

We heard a sucking noise, like boots emerging from a swamp as, almost simultaneously, the loch surged. Fin-shaped waves were spreading out from its heart, coiling like the limbs of a giant squid to flood what was left of the bank. Some yelled and began walking backwards to escape the overflow. Grown bold now, the guitar players lifted their instruments like clubs and looked out over the water, ready to act. But there was nothing to act against: just more sound, like groaning, the press of insistent, ground-covering waves. Children clasped whatever hand was prepared to take theirs and a helicopter reared into view like a black Pegasus, the pilot waving one arm from the cockpit. BACK, he mouthed, circling once, MOVE BACK, though only a handful could have seen before the harsh, warm gust that meant he had turned away for the last time. As the water groaned again and the copter disappeared, I wheeled, dragging my legs as though walking underwater. Perhaps I was afraid. A great belch of mud and gas behind me was all it took to convince my legs, of their own voli-tion, choosing at least a canter as my best chance. Where were the pheasants? Here only yesterday, now not one remained. On either side, tethered dogs strained on their leashes, part of the debris, the litter we would not come back for. Children were crying, separated already. Maybe their parents had left them behind. It was then, as I lurched uphill and away from whatever it was that headed towards us, I saw it. Off to my right, glowing in the dark, dry grass.

A tiny, living fire. I slowed.

Orange with coal-black flecks and magnesium-flare markings, those tiger-tints of amber, auburn, gold. Closer to, though I tried to still myself, the creature fluttered, showing its full colours. A copper Lycaenidae, but which? Its antennae, glowing like incense sticks, that frill, like bead-work on his wings; those distinctive legs. It was a Duke of Burgundy for sure. Male, perfect, impossibly far from home. Despite the situation, I surged with pleasure. An allegedly extinct butterfly. Yet here it was, miles from what had once been thought his normal habitat, breathing after all. More than breathing. Searching for a mate. And where he had chosen to search, where his instinct had driven him to best survive, was north. Beasts know things. They have not our choices, our disastrous tendency to self-will. And this beast chose north. As I watched, he folded himself in half and lifted weightlessly into the air, spiralling higher with every beat of his wings. Against all judgement, I waited, wishing him luck, till he disappeared.

Someone – more than one – crushed against me, insistent, haring in what I knew for sure now was the wrong direction. Trusting everything to an insect, I let his fitter senses guide me and took the left fork. I accelerated north, braced for solitude, defence of what little I needed, what little I deserved. Who knew what there might be, given healing time, given nature took the quickest route. I headed north.

opera

Splashing and gurgles in the throat. Listen.

A radio fast-forwarding channels. Not at all. It's Lola singing:

Love is just like the wildest bird that none can ever hope to tame

Some horrible translation she must have read somewhere chimes round the bright blue tiles, yearning rising with the steam. Lola can't see the steam because her eyes are shut. In the dark, she doesn't have to see how tired her breasts look, how many stomachs may emerge out of the bath clouds without warning. Blind, aqueous, she can be a wild slip of a thing, Carmen with scarlet fingernails rolling a cigar on her inner thigh, crazed with passion. *And if I love you, then beware of me!* Mouth opening on the flat of the water surface just below the island of her nose, a disembodied yawn, a singing puddle. At the end of the verse, she sings the accompaniment too, her chest cavity imagining a panther pulse of cellos, the announcement she is not done yet. She's turning like a bull to the matador, pawing towards the reprise. Her hands surface, clutch the edges of the bath like spiders, and there she is, risen from the suds like Venus, wrists high above her head playing absent castanets. Rivulets of water run like swollen veins down the length of her torso, her sodden, bruisy arms. *Carmencita* to the life.

L'amour est un oiseau rebelle qui nul ne peut apprivoiser

This time in French – the kind of French that could pass for Swedish, maybe, but it's close enough for Lola. Lola doesn't speak any foreign languages and can't sing like they do at the opera, can't sing even in tune. And she doesn't care. It's not for anyone else, after all: this is solely for Lola, for the physical joy of yodelling at the sky. No one is here to know. The bathroom is full of condensation and the door is locked. Lola had a whole packet of Jaffa Cakes all to herself, no sharing, the empty box there, evidence on the bath-side mat. Her soap smells of coconuts, her shampoo of papaya: the bath foam is kiwi fruit, macadamia nut and lime. Fruit-juice bubbles slick her hips, insinuate a frothy track between the crack of her buttocks. The bedroom is littered with cast-off clothes, the dishes aren't washed and there's nothing but tomato sauce in the fridge. But in here is another world and in here, Lola doesn't care about a damn thing, not about the brown stain still seeping through at the joins of the bathroom ceiling, about the stink of cats and beer piss at the front door, the pile of bills toasted curly on the top of the microwave – nothing. In here she is who she chooses to be and who she chooses is *Someone Fabulous.* *L'amour! L'amour!* she roars, pitching in the tub like a seal. Her breasts brush the enamel as she rolls on her front; the

mild abrasion of powder-bleach from the last time anyone
cleaned the bath burrs at her thighs but it doesn't put her
off. Not one bit. *L'amour!* she sings, big handles on her voice,
meaning it every time. At the climax, she surges, splashing
the cork-tile floor with spume. *Si je t'aime* – fixing one eye
on the figment of some anonymous man, she is a rebel,
a sex goddess, the icing on a fat, spiced cake – *si je t'aime
prends garde à toi!* And she stands up, holding the moment
inside the ringing echo of her own voice; woman incarnate,
a gypsy with blood on her lips. Look and you can see her
without much trying. Head flipped back like her neck just
broke. There's a bare lightbulb, a white-cold ceiling. Lola's
eyes, shiny as marbles.

Harmless. Kind of cute.

To pretend to be Carmen in private is not a fault. Michaela
doesn't think so either – she likes it. Michaela's just the
lodger, presently in the front room straightening cushions.
A minute ago she was all ears, but the stopped singing in
the bathroom at the end of the hall kicked her off into a
tidy fit, a child caught daydreaming by the teacher. For the
silence means one thing: Lola is about the act of drying. Ten
minutes more and she'll be in the living room, turbaned
and pink and wondering where her perfume is *dammit
dammit leave my things alone Michaela stop tidying my bloody
things away* – turning the place Michaela has taken pains
to tidy into a fresh mess before she finds it, where she left
it all along. After that, she digs out a row of bullet-shaped
lipsticks and that black lycra cocktail dress, one meant for

somebody smaller, the one that clings to every nook and cranny, and files her hips as she pulls it up with her fingers straining, snapping the spaghetti-thin straps in place as her finale. Gorgeous, she'll dust off the white marks that show the struggle, run her hands over the Reubens bump of her belly. No tummy-control knickers for Lola. No knickers at all. Real men, she says, like proper curves. They don't like bumps on a woman's arse where the elastic makes a ghost under your frock. They like beauty-spots, extra eyelashes and cherry-stained lips and they get those as well. A night out is a tight-rope, Lola says, but she can walk it. Sandals with peep-toes and heels in all weathers: forearms hand-cuffed with silver bangles, ears sliced through with dangly hoops. Her hair, flicked out, flicked up, pinned up, pinned out, curled loose or at the tipping point of tight: she runs her fingers through the soft, warm paste she makes herself from beeswax to set it neat. She tips the ends of her fringe to curls on her forehead, makes little fronds like ivy down the long slope of her neck. *Like I just got out of bed*, she says. *And no hairspray – Michaela, jeez have you tasted the bloody stuff?*

And Michaela never says *who's going to taste your hair, Lola? Who does that?* With the best of intentions she just keeps mum. That's the girl, she says. You stick with me, and learn something.

Michaela has no doubt it's true. She watches Lola pat her lips with toilet paper, slicks a second coat of colour, pouts like a fish: Michaela knows every stage that goes into the making of this persona, into the making of what Lola is in the outside world. Splendid. Something to be reckoned with. Solid gold.

Whose place is this? Who found it, furnished it, tricked it out? Who pays the rent? Who shares wine that tastes like lighter fuel and writes MINE in marker pen on the insides of her shoes? Who puts out milk for strays? *Who do you think?* All Michaela has to do is take the odd phone call, keep the kitchen nice, stock the fridge now and then from the corner shop so there's more than crisps and salsa and not get in the way. She's embarrassed by how little it is, but Lola's the boss and she won't have more. She deals with the sprawl and noise, the men in the close at night, spoiling for fights; the cats that call and spatter the concrete close with piss. Wherever her money comes from (and Michaela isn't sure), it's Lola handles running costs, says it costs her just the same when Michaela isn't there and won't respond to offers. *I don't pry*, she says: *and neither do you. That's the deal.* They don't talk family, childhood, friends. All Michaela knows for sure is what she sees and what she sees is this. First, that Lola found her – a stranger with the feel of the Irish ferry still under her feet, a split-sided suitcase and some phone camera snaps for company. And second, even when she told the truth about her age at the third time of asking, Michaela got to stay.

Overnight at first, slowly, over days. Three weeks now and Michaela is still fifteen but older in the head. She has a friend who knows things. A friend who tells the future. It's not a trick. At weekends, sometimes weekday nights, she reads their cards and cups, the destiny lines on their hands. Women – nearly always women – come up the cold stone stairs and knock, and Lola sits them on her black velvet cushions and makes them tea. She ties her hair up in a scarf, not costumed up like Hallowe'en. She looks like Lola. *You've got to take it serious, she says. Folk are desperate these days and that's the truth. If they need to believe it, I believe it as well. You can't not.*

Other days big brown boxes come in vans and Lola stacks them in a cupboard at the back of the flat, taps her nose, smiles. *The grey economy,* she says, *c'est moi.* And late at night, most nights, Lola goes out; her coat over her shoulder, nowhere specific, nobody's business but her own. Some nights she's chirpy, some nights she looks worn out, but she goes anyway. *You're only young once,* she says. *You can sleep when you're dead.* And shuts the door. Michaela listens to the sound of her heels, the kiss she blows over her shoulder as she disappears out of the street light, heading for a bus. And Michaela tries. Who wants to be a miseryguts? She makes an effort not to wait up, not to worry if Lola doesn't come back, sometimes for days. She doesn't phone or go out looking: it's not her business. *I can look after myself,* Lola says. *The last thing I need is a ball and chain. Don't even think about it.* And Michaela, knowing her place, stays home in it, shuts up, waits.

The city is no place for someone soft. Sometimes she thinks she might even go back where she came from, take the boat the other way. But not yet. She can't go home

without Aidan. At least knowing where he is. Head for
the city and start asking, they'd said. Take your photo and
ask. Only it hadn't dawned before she saw the city how
different it would be, how terrifying, how not up to it she'd
feel confronted with strangers who spoke so differently,
laughed at stuff she didn't understand and anyway, had
their own problems. By not going back but hanging on
here, Michaela was beginning to wonder if it meant she
was hoping, not consciously but in a sneakier, underhand
way, that Lola would do it for her. Big capable Lola with her
nose for things, her fearless eye-to-eye would take over the
dirty work and track him down for her. She had known the
story from the first night, or at least most of it, even without
trying. *Let's read your cards, pet: a bit of fun* and it came out
card by card, ridiculously tiny little glass of sherry by glass
of sherry. It tasted like sweeties and Michaela had two, in
thrall to what the cards said. It hadn't seemed possible that
a stranger knew how to unravel so much. So easily.

Man, Lola said, tapping at the pack with her nail; no surprise. Dark hair? Tower. He's trouble. Hanged Man – that's
a fool's errand. You know what this means?

Michaela knew what it meant. After, she understood
Lola was making up what she suspected from watching,
just taking in the semaphore Michaela was sending out.
But at the time, it seemed there was no hiding from what a
supernatural agency had confessed for her. When the first
deal was finished, Lola turned over two more; *rounding off,
she said. Just putting on the tin lid.* Seven of Cups, Queen of

Coins. But Lola didn't say what they meant. She said they added nothing new and bundled them together, done. Then she reached across the table and stroked Michaela's cheek. Her touch was light – a warm glide of slippery-smooth nail varnish against her skin, Lola's whisper reaching her ear.

Why him, eh? What's so special about one man?

Michaela, with no answer, said nothing. That wasn't the point of the question. The point of the question was raising the question at all. Lola folded the cards between her thumbs, shuffled them with a single flick.

We've all got to want something, eh? Even if it's no good.

Michaela did not drink the last of her sherry. Looking at its blood-brown colour through the glass, tilting the thick last drop like sand in an egg-timer, Michaela, already lightheaded, asked something she shouldn't.

So what about yourself? She heard herself saying it. What is it you want, Lola? It must be something. Everyone wants something.

As Lola looked back, Michaela thought *I've done it now. I'm out on my ear.* But Lola wasn't angry. She opened out a square of velvet cloth, folded her deck of carefully shuffled futures away, then pushed back in her chair, kicked her shoes off, spoke.

One thing, since you're asking, she said. Just one, mind.

Michaela looked up, tentative, saw Lola looking back, her head settling back into the cushion, almost serene.

I want a grand finale. An unforgettable last act. A finale to die for.

Then she drew back her head and laughed. And laughed. And laughed.

Michaela hadn't known what to make of it at the time and said nothing. Lola, still smiling, had simply reapplied her eyeliner and gone out, earlier than usual. She might as well have written a message in pan stick on the bathroom mirror: *The Subject is Closed*.

Now, all these weeks later, Michaela still doesn't know what to think and doesn't try too hard. She hopes she didn't hurt Lola's feelings: Lola was not the kind who would ever admit such a thing possible. Wondering now, as she sits alone in the flat, Michaela still has no clear idea what it is Lola wants for her life, if anything. She has watched her only friend in this place swilling tea dregs, going through her repertoire for clients wondering the most personal things imaginable; watched those clients in no doubt Lola knew something they didn't. She has felt privileged to be here. She has watched Lola stashing boxes into the always-locked back room and listened to her singing in the bath, perfectly at ease with herself in the here and now. And she has totted up the fragments of advice Lola has given her and not given her, wondered sometimes if Lola is in fact addressing no one but herself. *Do what you want with your life, you don't get another one. Never apologise, never explain. Stay light, stay free. Jealousy kills; it kills whatever it touches.* And thinking it, Michaela feels something spoiling the place inside her head where Lola lives out her fairy-godmother existence; something increasingly difficult, now she sees with fresh eyes, to ignore.

For as well as its charmed circle, Lola shares her life with other people too. Shadowy people glimpsed fleetingly or not at all; just voices heard behind doors or on the phone if Michaela picks it up because she's the only one home; now and then, the coat on a man's back as it flutters down the stairwell never once looking back. Maybe Lola says exactly the same things to these people too. *Never apologise, never explain.* And to begin with, they think they like it. *Stay light, stay free.* They see the advantages, their chance to have what Lola is with no strings, no complications. Then they find she expects the same. That when she says *no* she really means it. Guys who can't believe their luck till the day they come round looking for her and find she's out in that tight dress but not with them, that she's pulling other men because it's fun she's after, not a lost sheep. Guys Lola calls *their own worst enemies,* but puts herself out for anyway because it's what she does. Until its enough. Until you're ready to take your life back.

One day, Michaela thinks, one of them might be a man who doesn't know till it happens he's the jealous type. Now and then, when Lola isn't in, Michaela has heard the phone ring till it cuts off again, again, again; long messages of awful, needy silence till she hangs up to make it go away. And Michaela has almost said something already, but knows Lola won't take her seriously. *You're worse than him, kid,* she'll say, opening the door with one hand, the bruise on her arm patched with concealer and fake tan. *I'm a big girl. If you're so worried, watch tv. Get a kitten. Or stop me. On you go.* That lush red smile, knowing Michaela couldn't stop a bus, never mind a runaway train like Lola. That smile Lola turns on when you try to care for her that used to make Michaela laugh with pleasure but now does not. These days, Michaela watches Lola testing her face in the hallway mirror, drawing a temporary tattoo, a line of barbed wire, round the stalk of her neck and that smile can chill her right to the bone. *Stop me. On you go.* Michaela is afraid to think how wild a man who was his own worst enemy might become by her being simply the kind of woman she is. By being the kind of woman he can't have.

Thinking further than that is something she doesn't want to do at all.

And if I love you, then beware!

Last one.

The singing has stopped now.

No more of her two languages, no more locked in behind a closed door. She is rehearsing instead for a night on the tiles, will say *Well you have to don't you* on the grounds she's a long time dead. It's irrefutable. You are.

Michaela plumps the cushions and keeps listening to Lola, silently now, preparing to hit the town. She folds away a magazine, brushes crumbs from the side-table, piles CDs into a flaky stack. Michaela doesn't want to see Lola cinching her wrists and ears with metal, hanging her ears with hooks; checking her face in the mirror, brittle as Tiffany glass. She doesn't want to see what card she flips over before she leaves. But she will. She bets she will. She'll watch

Lola pick up Aidan's picture that makes the wallpaper on Michaela's phone, hear that tease in her voice that's almost a dare – green eyes, kid, he's got green eyes. Then the door will click; Lola's heels will echo in the stone stairwell. Kid, she'll shout, loud enough for the whole close to hear, a parting shot – I bet I find him before you do. And she'll laugh. At the bottom of the stairwell, she'll laugh, trailing the last line of her favourite song like Havana smoke, heading towards the curtain.

romantic

He's there when I arrive, twenty minutes late, still standing at the bar. I can tell from his face he's ordered already and he doesn't kiss me hello. He usually consents to a kissed hello, but I am late again. I don't deserve it.

Sorry, Charlie, I say. Traffic.

I know, he says. It's always traffic. Anyway, I've ordered.

I know.

This – he says grandly, opening one arm like a theatre curtain – is Maria. She's Hungarian. He nods in a *don't make a fuss* sort of a way. She's just staying over for a few days at the flat.

There are always people staying over at the flat. We have that kind of place. I smile at Maria and her long blue hair, her dark purple nails. She smiles back with a look that suggests she is fed up being smiled at by strangers and having her hair noticed. It's probably been happening all day and she's tired. Maybe she's just arrived.

She's tired, Charlie says. Just arrived.

I smile again. We were going to have a meal out at the

bar together, nothing fancy, but just me and Charlie. We don't do it often and we save up, look forward. For entertainment, I brought some self-help book Simon wants him to review for the *Herald* and pictures of funny cats off the internet as light relief in case work is a no-go area over dinner. I thought we'd have a beer and a laugh, but not now. Maria is both here and Hungarian, so couples-out-for-a-night-together in-jokes and self-help books are not suitable conversation. Charlie says he ordered Cullen Skink and haggis to do his bit for Scottish tourism and Maria looks blank. He likes haggis anyway, but he's making a self-deprecating joke for either me or Maria – which is hard to say – suggesting her ethnic origins are being indulged to placate an unexpressed requirement for local guidance.

Charlie is a self-appointed Statue of Liberty: the poor, huddled masses and foreigners know. The way moths find light. I'm never sure whether he enjoys cherishing the stranger in his midst or if it's a compulsion. He's always been an earnest sort, more earnest as he ages. It used to be very attractive.

Anyhow, I make travelling small-talk to Maria to be helpful and give him a breather and he uses it to scan the room and start waving. Charlie spends a lot of his waking hours waving, mostly at people he doesn't know. A friend I haven't met yet – that sort of thing. Even before the wave stops he buggers off to speak to some different woman in ripped tights on the other side of the bar. I notice she gets the kiss I didn't get and ask Maria how she likes Edinburgh, enunciating more clearly than usual so she can tune in to the new accent.

It's ok.

I nod. This is Edinburgh, the Athens of the North, we're talking about here; Edinburgh is apparently *ok*.

Not as nice as Budapest.

No, I say. Budapest is unique.

Yes, she says. Everywhere is. That's a truism.

And we're done. Charlie comes back just as Maria is discovering she hates Cullen Skink, so he eats his alone while she goes outside for a fag to take the taste away and I can't see her through the window. Either she's had enough or she's shorter than I thought.

Nervous of butting in, Charlie says. He means Maria. She thinks we're business partners, not – well, whatever the word is these days. I called you my partner and she assumed it wasn't a personal thing. You know, like *business partner.* He shrugs, picks haddock from between his teeth with a nail. The buzz all around us gets louder. More people are coming in to eat. I'm just about to order myself a beer since nobody else will when Ruaridh breezes in, all rippling tee-shirt and bouncy as a pup. He says hi, clocks I have no drink and orders one for me too. All one move; the way tall guys seem so fluently to be able to do, over my head before the barmaid even spots me. I smile at him, feeling the best I have since I came in and he rests a hand on my shoulder. Maria turns up dead on cue, wondering if she and Charlie are about to go to the garden where the castle is (she has heard the castle is very romantic) and Charlie, no hesitation, dumps cash on the bar for the waiter.

Tell them no thanks for the haggis, he says. You appear to be staying.

And that's it. Gone. All I have to do is make sure Charlie's uneaten feast is no longer a burden and spend the afternoon with Ruaridh, cheered up by how square his jaw is, how green his eyes are after a pint or two. I can't hold it these days.

I can't get the hang of English girls, he says. Glad to be back. A load of talk about cars and food and *my new project*. They take work so fucking seriously down there!

Well, sounds like the ones you met do.

Another thing, he says, not listening to me, is they take it so fucking seriously when you say fuck a lot. Like they think it's swearing or something.

We laugh. He's young in the head even for a young thing. And good-looking. He's really good-looking.

I like intelligent women, he said. Looks are nothing. What's sexy is smart. Guys that don't get that are fucking morons. He smiled. Only problem is, the intelligent ones pack you in quicker. Just been dumped.

Oh, I say. Sad face. You ok?

Terrible, he says. Distraught and all that. Let's not talk about it.

He smiles again. This time I smile back. We smile too long.

So, he says. Want to share a cab?

I look at him. You don't know where I live.

No, he said. You could come back to mine. It's an invitation.

I look at him.

I'd nearly forgotten what a great place it is. Big bay window, lovely view of the castle. You'd like it.

I laugh. Castle view. Expensive.

Well, he says, when I say you can see the castle I mean you can see the castle if you stand on the bed, jump up and down a wee bit. But still. Romantic.

He is looking at his feet. Almost blushing. Then he lifts his head and our eyes lock. Just long enough.

What do you say? he says. Welcome me home.

I keep looking at him, widen my eyes. He is nearly twenty years younger than me. Peridot green-eyed. So bloody good-looking. My shoulders ripple. The hairs on the back of my neck rise.

Sure, I say. I have under-appreciated cats on my mobile if we run out of things to say. Get-out clause – in case.

Outside, he touches the back of my neck. We kiss.

You sure? I say.

Sure I'm sure, he says. No expectations. See what you think when we get there. It's too big a bed for one.

So we walk. Bugger the cab, we take our time. We walk.

Tonight the pub can keep its waifs, its strays, its temporary friends and noise. Fleetingly, I imagine pissed-off

Maria finding Edinburgh disappointing, noticing Charlie's teeth spiked here and there with slivers of fish. This time of night, in the right company, I hear the castle is very romantic.

peak

All attraction was based on a flaw of logic. I knew that.

Miss Bennet and Mr Darcy, Scarlett and Rhett, Edward Rochester and the wife in the attic whose name hardly anyone recalls because what is she to the plot save a complication? But I did it anyway.

The Singles Valentine Night was a first for the Psychology Department. I already knew my worst enemy was mistrust, which is unhelpful when *looking for love.* I'm not an idiot. I knew Singles Valentine Night was code for Speed-Dating for Divorced Academics who have Almost Forgotten what Sex for Two is like. But I also knew that reluctance to properly try was exactly the kind of self-defeating bloody-mindedness that got me here in the first place. So, dragging my not-trying-too-high heels I went forth with a grim determination that would soon become an open mind. How hard could it be?

The Speed-Dating How-To postcards at the door were all gone by the time I arrived, and I scraped in just before the welcome speech, my first avoidance tactic outfoxed.

Some guy was giving a short reassurance there was nothing wrong with us for being here, followed by an even shorter how-to: gentlemen to remain seated throughout/ each meet should begin with two personal statements each to spring-board conversation/ladies move on to the next table at the bell. A man with a well-groomed beard had already occupied his preferred table and set up two glasses and a bottle not far from where I was standing; unstressed, roughly the same age as me give or take and not obviously creepy. So I licked my teeth and zeroed in on the starting pistol. Bang.

Eugene, he said. As in Eugene Onegin.

Pushkin, I said. Kills Lensky, doesn't get the girl.

Only more contemporary, haha, he said. I have no Russian blood, so it would turn out different with me. He turned his name card round. Eugene, it said. Absurdism: Kierkegaard to Camus. He held out a hand and we shook.

I'm Simone as in De Beauvoir and I know more than I'd like about the central nervous system, so we have something in common.

What do you do? he said.

I'm a psychiatrist, I said. I've heard every shrink joke there is. But I'm not a shrink. I'm a psychiatrist. Don't try to be funny.

Wow, he said. What does being here say about us? He looked concerned.

It says we have less than three minutes to go, I said. You first. And off he went.

He wanted *to do what he wanted to do* not *what he was supposed to do* while there was still time. Taking a risk, not undermining himself in advance and not blaming himself if it all went wrong, etc.

So many of us are alone these days from simple inhibition now there aren't any rules, he said. That's my time up. Now you.

Well, I said. I think I'm probably anxious we have no rules either to follow or break, too. I breathed in slowly, breathed out. Sorry. It's my first time doing anything like this.

Me too, he said. I'm hoping I don't sound too matter-of-fact.

You're doing fine, I said. You haven't asked me if I'm going to analyse you and that's a plus. Analysts, even for analysands, are still a source of not-very-funny jokes.

Really? he said.

Yup, I nodded. It's a defensive thing: a fear they might say something that sounds crazy and I'll make assumptions. I've been doing it so long now, they might be on to something. Who's to say?

We smiled. We may have laughed for no good reason. Then the bell rang. Recalling what the ladies had been instructed to do on that trigger, I stood, shook his hand and he slipped me a card. His card. His phone number. His name.

Our first meet-up was at a sushi bar just off Chambers Street where we chose chopsticks to show our willingness to be off-the-leash. We did not say anything obviously defensive and did not drink. We managed a slightly-self-conscious-touching-hands-while-walking thing as we left, but both avoided any kiss finale. Why would we kiss because we had a Japanese meal? Because people in your situation do, I told myself going upstairs. It's a nod to sub-text. They just do.

Date two was his place: he didn't drive and I had a car. I got to his front door out of breath from three flights of stairs and waited to get my breath back. But it had to be obvious I was there. I sounded like a Labrador.

Hi! he said, opening the door. He looked cool as get-out in pristine pale grey dressing gown, loose white shirt and trousers. His feet were bare.

You found me, he said. It came out thrilled. We sort-of embraced and he pointed at the bare feet. Putting my money where my mouth is about *being myself*. I do this all the time I'm at home. If it's creepy let me know.

It's not creepy, I said. The gown isn't black towelling with soup stains, it's beautiful. Guys in short dressing gowns – that's creepy.

Not sure whether I was joking, he gave me a brief introduction to the hallway. Kitchen door, bathroom door, cupboard for the washing machine, living room. And the exit, he said, pointing behind me, is where you just came in.

I nodded. He was not making a joke.

The three-minute bell thing was great, he said.

Didn't you think? Stopped us from talking too much or pissing about.

I hope we're not timing this evening, I said.

Haha of course not, he said. Just an observation. I think that initial night was more spontaneous than sushi night. Anyway, you look great.

He slipped behind me to assist coat-removal. I emerged wearing my going-out black dress with sleeves and kicked off my shoes to look more casual next to his dressing-down thing.

You too, I said, having to tilt my head up to where his eyes were. I had these shoes on both times we met. You probably had no idea I was this small.

You don't paint your toenails! he said. He sounded excited.

No, I said. Not since I was thirteen. How about you?

But he was already loading the coat into the laundry cupboard, so I looked around, taking in the vista. Nearest was an academic's living room, few surprises. Lots of books, some on shelves, some on a table in the window, some on the floor, plug-in air fresheners to dilute the smell of the older books and music playing low in the background. Not André Rieu, thank god and not Pink Floyd: and not anything so engrossing I'd give up on conversation altogether just to listen. Good start. The coat tucked away near the washing machine, he took us both inside the living room and my feet sank into a shag-pile rug deep as a walk on the beach. Set out on the heirloom side-table was a plate of shop-bought sandwiches cut into fingers, a bunch of fat black grapes and three bottles of red and two of spirits on the lower rack. Yes to two glasses, not more, I told myself: you'll only fall asleep.

He opened out his hand as if introducing me to the sofa and I sat. Soft, expensive, no cushions. Leaning back was like bouncing on a mattress. He took the armchair opposite, squirrelling his toes into the shag pile like a boy. I was, I admit it, charmed.

Across the narrow table we ate fancy salmon, shrimp and mixed-cheese sandwiches and talked tv drama, the *New Statesman*'s failure to grasp that Scotland exists, the fraud of trickle-down economics, the decline of literary fiction, dementia and whether sex was in decline because of internet pornography, fear or boredom. An app called NOT THAT ONE made us lean closer for a moment to share mutual revulsion of contemporary dating patterns and the sadness of peering at a screen pre-loaded with strangers. Neither of us had tried it. Besides, he observed, phones were germ-ridden sewers.

I noticed he held his phone inside a handkerchief just before he wiped it down, slid it along the leg of his trousers and switched it off. I turned back to the grapes to avoid commenting on his germ phobia and took one.

So, I said. You listen to music.

Wow, he said. I hadn't even noticed it stopped. I have Ella Fitzgerald right here.

He walked backwards to the sound box, pressed a key, and there she was, almost in person, rolling out of the hidden speakers. Who doesn't like jazz?

That's not jazz, I said. It's Cole Porter. Lost the use of his legs and experienced years of pain before he died at the age of seventy-three feeling he had failed.

It's Ella Fitzgerald, he said. That's all that counts. Let's face the music?

I laughed. I won't dance, don't ask me. But you can pour me another glass – one more is my limit.

I held out the empty and, for what I realised was the first time, smiled properly. He reached for the bottle and leaned towards me.

Actually, he said, slowly filling in my pink-tinted glass, I have an idea. He set the bottle down. You know what I'd really like to do?

No, I said gingerly. I looked at the floor.

I'd like to run you a nice, relaxing bath. I looked at him.

I run a good bath, he said. You won't be disappointed. I may even have made a little preparation in the hope you'd say yes.

He went out for a moment, came back with another dressing down over his arm. See, he said. I've put some thought into it.

I put my hand on the folded towelling. It was plush, peach-coloured and just as soft, smelling of brand new.

It'll be fun, he said. It's not about getting you to undress, not really. It's just about – well – you remember the freeing-up thing. Like we talked about. Doing something without overthinking. Spontaneously. Unless—

Ok, I said. Why not? Why not?

I undressed listening to the taps running full-on next door, hoping I'd lose any compression marks from my underwear under the gown. *We didn't have to do anything we didn't want to do*, I told myself. *It's only a bath. I could easily take him in a fight.*

But I undressed. I put on the dressing gown. It felt wonderful. Like velvet. He came back in.

Wow, he said. I knew it would suit you. They suit everybody.

He poured more wine, sat close. We clinked. Ella turned up 'Let's Face the Music and Dance' and we were all set. I'll show you the way, he said. We could take our drinks. He kissed my cheek. And I have another idea.

Oh? I said.

What he wanted, he said, what he had wanted *for some time*, to be honest, was to watch a woman shaving her legs.

Pause.

Warm bath, bubbles up to the armpits like a 70s Cadbury advert, pale toenails, a touch of lipstick, totally relaxed. But she's not alone. *He* would be there too. *He* would be there with the *express permission* of the woman in question to be an observer while she lay back in the bubbles, completely relaxed. And – this is the thing, he said, it's not for *him*. It's for her. It's a symbol of the woman's total control of the situation and her generosity in sharing.

By now, the radiant display from the fire had made the wine so red it was black. It wasn't too weird and anyway, spontaneity was the point. Still, it surprised me. Was it demeaning? Was it just icky? Did it count as spontaneous if he'd planned it? Or was it indeed exactly what I said I had wanted – a chance to be *less pointlessly cerebral*? Freeing myself up a little, this time not by crying at a sad thing on tv alone but with another human being in an effort to deliberately relax? It didn't sound unattractive and I'd had two full glasses of very good red. I was not remotely tipsy. Or not much. He topped up the present glass as I sat there, thinking.

Give me a moment, I said. I'm letting the idea sink in.

Sure, he said. Take your time. After a moment of silence, he inched closer, reached to the cloth where the dressing gown had slipped from one shoulder and touched it with his lips. You're in charge.

Then, from his trouser pocket, he held up a tiny bottle of nail varnish; a rose-pink sphere with a black screw-top he must have stowed away when he was next door, fiddling with the taps. He rotated the top of the bottle.

That's the important thing, he said. You're in charge.

My head filled with the lavender and jasmine clouds from the bathroom. Closer to, the acetate tang of varnish, a smell I identified with glamour ever since I was small, bloomed in my nose the way it had when I was a girl.

Eugene was holding the bottle, in case. I shut my eyes, the better to be in the moment, and spoke the words slowly and without hesitation.

Unleash the paint, I said. Stripe me pink. I met his gaze. Let's do it.

I was tipsy, but not stupid. His bathroom was pure white, pressure-steamer clean, the bath itself piled high with a thick meringue of bubbles, some the size of snowballs. Over the sink, a theatrical mirror shone a surround of bulbs. Warm, I loosened the belt of the gown, then hesitated. I wanted a few stage-directions, I said. What was his role? He would sit in the furthest corner, he said. Out of the way. Unless directly addressed, he would be silent; a watcher by permission only. He would turn his back while I got in, so I could take my time, acclimatise. Then wait till I told him when he might turn round, if at all.

Just take your time, he said. Unwind. I'm an optional extra.

Trust-games? I asked. Trust-games, he said. He turned his back and walked into the corner of the bathroom, near the now-closed door.

I took two steps, slid a hand through the foam to find where the water level might be, then dropped the peach gown to step into the tub, glad he had his back to me. In, I managed to turn and lie back comfortably without squeaking against the resin or any danger of drowning. He had judged the water level so well, I didn't even have to dip down to hide my nipples. I found myself sighing as I leaned back, the water touching my chin. I almost laughed at how good it felt.

Good? he asked. His back was still turned.

Yes, good, I said. I raised one arm as if reaching for the ceiling tiles, let the foam slither down my arms. I didn't look in his direction – of course not, he wasn't supposed to be *there* – but saw him from the corner of my eye turning to sit on the clean white tiles and rest his back against the wall for comfort, his eyes still closed. Testing, I stretched a single foot all the way to the taps, watched the suds slither round my leg like creeping vines. In the bath-rack, a brand-new bar of soap, shaving foam, and pink-handled, easy-grip safety razor had been set out. Fully loaded, ready to go. Since I shave my legs less than seldom and had something to bring to the party, I thought the least I could do was join in. I lifted the shaving foam, eased off the lid.

Then, despite the unfamiliarity of the surroundings and occasion, allowed the next move to find itself.

I paid attention to the angle of the blade. Slicing into the thin skin of the ankle would discolour the bathwater, be vaguely repulsive and stop any aspect of fun either of us might find in doing this in the first place, so I took my time. I bathed my arms to raise my general temperature, then folded forward, stretching out one foot, toes pointed, to a reachable height with the rest of me still warm behind the white froth. Then, with just enough foam in the palm of one hand, I lathered my skin from knee to Achilles tendon, then reached for the pink disposable. Long strokes for long stretches of skin, feather strokes in corners – more caution than instinct. It was soothing in more ways than one to focus on something so trivial yet demanding of attention. Done, I bathed the first leg and heard him ask if he could open his eyes.

If you want, I said. But stay where you are. I'm very keenly focused right now. I breathed deep and raised the next lower limb. The man in the corner could be himself and I could be myself at the same time. It was vaguely freeing. And I wasn't done. I lathered my armpits gently, shaved them too, tiny feather strokes. Then on impulse and without looking in his direction, I found myself saying, Eugene? Do you still have the varnish?

He stood up slowly, soundlessly and held up the bottle. I saw from the corner of an eye without directly looking into his eyes.

Toenails, I smiled. Just for the hell of it.

Ok, he said. If you're inviting me, ok.

He approached and waited. Can I touch your arm?

I offered my wrist, still without meeting his eyes, and felt him kiss the inner skin where the veins rise pale blue to the surface. Then he lifted my arm higher and closer, kissing his way towards my armpit; first softly, then deeper when he heard me catch my breath. I slid back when he was done, my now-wet hair coiled round my neck like a collar, and offered my right foot for painting.

Oh wow, he said, cupping my ankle, setting the varnish bottle on the sill. These are the toes of a real woman, Simone. My god, they're hairy.

It was true. I've always had interesting toes. He sat on

the bath edge placing my wet sole on his thighs where it slopped a trail of bubbles over his crotch like saliva.

I mean, *really* hairy. These legs of yours like stripped pine after paring, then *this* – he caught his breath – like the toes of a chimp or something, a humanoid, a half-wild beast.

He looked at my face, then drew my foot closer, poking his tongue into the spaces between each toe again and again and again and again till I felt goosebumps on my nipples, saw his lips darken as his blood-flow notched up. This was wholly new to me. My entire skin surface was rippling. The climax caught me out. I quite literally didn't see it coming. Then he slowed, stopped, patted my toes dry, and brushed each of my toenails with smooth brush-lines of soft pink sealant then blew softly to help them dry.

Done, he helped me stand up and held a freshly laundered towel to dry myself with, another to conceal myself if I wanted. I wanted. My skin was beginning to cool. Oblivious, he knelt and rubbed my legs and arms with oil that smelled of freesias to soothe the shaven skin, and told me he had an idea for one final detail. I saw a blade between his finger and thumb, just the blade, fresh edged, no holder.

Final?

Final.

You're not going to shave my toes, I said.

He smiled. No, Simone. I'm going to shave something else. Those shadowy sideburns the same colour as your hair are one thing. But I want more. I want the barely visible down of your perfect upper lip, those baby shoots of woman-stubble. I want—

—but I didn't much care for what he wanted. Not any more.

Maybe it was the overworked sentences. Maybe the wine was wearing off. Maybe his theatricality was beginning to show. Or maybe I just wanted to go to sleep.

Thanks, I said. But I want to go home.

Underwear, shoes, no skimping, I dressed slower than I undressed and that told me something too. I could fetch the car tomorrow, sober. I watched the light in his upstairs window from the back of the cab, the vague shape of him pulling the blinds and enjoyed that we'd done what we set out to do.

How many people can say that? Now, our capacity for self-deception must be recognised and acted upon. If I learned one thing from Sartre, it was that transformation is fleeting and this kind most of all. We'd peaked.

distance

The deer came down to the road at night, slipping through the bracken just before dusk. By sundown, more beasts than seemed natural would reach the tarmac, sure-footing their way across to the narrow beach. They were there that first night, pallid in the headlights as she rolled off the ferry, turning to watch her as she slowed to a stall. Every night since, using petrol it would probably have been wiser to save, she had come back to see them do it again. They paid little attention to her, just went about their business, picking their way to the sand, their young close beside them. Sometimes, they turned and sniffed the air, then ambled slowly on. Something primitive, she guessed, was drawing them. Her too. Deer did not judge, did not speculate about her motives: they simply were. And so, they decided, was she. Gentle things made bolder by the dying light, they met her eye to eye, their pupils huge, absorbent in the dark. This was their element, not hers. But she had permission to stay.

Martha had not expected to be so struck by any of it. That the island would be beautiful she had taken for granted.

That was what Scottish Islands were, after all: heather and bracken, tumbledown crofts and Highland cows, solitary eagles, hovering over rugged grandeur.

And water: streams to waterfalls, crashing waves – a lot of water. That the place was entirely as perfect as expected surprised her nonetheless. Even late in the year, the lushness was heart-stopping: a small continent of greens and russets, clumps of bramble, fern and rush grass fringed by seaweed, scrub and scree. The window of the hotel bedroom framed a tethered boat that never seemed to move, red hull twinned against the mirror-surface sea. Most mornings, a seal twisted his way between the scattered rocks of the Small Isles. That she could not identify the birds that hung like dancers over the harbour did not matter: they'd be there tomorrow, and every day after that whether she knew what they were or not. She was superfluous. Finally harmless.

Peter was three when he split his head on a sheet glass table. She had been serving soup from a pot on the stove, heard him pattering closer in his socks and from instinct, looked up. The whole thing played before her in mere seconds in the shiny backboard of the cooker. He was running towards the table, laughing, then without warning came a dreadful crack like gunshot as the child stopped in his tracks, raising his hands to his face, his mouth wide. He crumbled to the floor as the howling started, the pain. Kneeling, trying to understand, she saw the blood:

like paint from the lip of a can, thick and scarlet. A towel pressed to his forehead soaked as soon as it touched, blood forcing up through the fibres. As though the wound beneath had been made by a cutlass. She cradled his face, hands running like a butcher's, as his eyes rolled and the screaming went on, and on, and on. If he was dying, she thought, bracing his little body tight, smiling down at him out of sheer terror; if he was bleeding to death, her duty was reassurance. As she pressed the right numbers slowly, carefully, into the phone with one hand, the other clutched him close, not letting go. As she spelled out their address to the operator, her voice clear, she kept her gaze steady, point to point on his. He would not be afraid because she was afraid. He would not be afraid.

It's all right, she crooned, as he shook, barely containable between her arms. I'm here. He rattled against her chest. Let mummy take it, she whispered. Let me take it instead.

After, it soothed her he could not have heard her. It would have been impossible for him to have heard what she had said.

At hospital, things were more detached. Cuts to the forehead, the nurse said; they always barked worse than they bit. She meant there was always lots of blood, often no lasting damage. They stitched him back together so gently, he fell asleep the minute it was done. Next afternoon, he woke woozy, heavy-lidded, but more or less himself. The table survived with only a minor crack and three stained towels were thrown away; Peter's torn skin mended behind a Cat in the Hat plaster and everything fell to rights again. Everything but Martha.

It started with dreams; formless things in empty rooms, black shapes worming towards her as she slept. More than once, a sensation of falling woke her sweating, fearful, as Riley slept, oblivious, beside her. Before long, she took to taping the empty slits of the electrical sockets in the skirting, shifting ornaments and glassware from reachable shelves. Toiletry bottles in the bathroom were swapped for plastic containers. She fit a brass lock on the cupboard full of bleaches, acids and cast fluids; removed the tea-towel hooks from Peter's eye-level at the sink. She put rubber bumpers on the edges of their softwood dining table, threw out a set of toy screwdrivers and long-handled paintbrushes as asking for trouble. Riley's penknife was removed from his key ring; the ancient tube tv – too big, too heavy – now sat on the floor. When she began waking Peter at night, checking more than once if he was breathing, Riley drew a line.

You've had a shock, but for godsake. He paused, softened his voice. You'll make Peter paranoid at this rate. The last thing we need is you being—

He looked at her, let his shoulders slump, then smiled, limply. Just don't go turning into your mother, eh?

The mention of her mother, even as a joke, was something

Martha hadn't seen coming. For all that, she knew what he meant. He thought she was being – what was it he had always called her? Neurotic Nancy. Neither of them ever called Martha's mother *mother*, but Riley, more often than not, attached the adjective. He had also called her – the words formed in her head as she looked at her husband now – a selfish old bitch who ruined your life. Under her gaze, Riley flinched.

Look, he said. I'm not trying to blame. He brushed the fringe out of her eyes. But it's time to get a grip, Martha. To move on.

Move on. Martha only realised she had said the words when she heard them out loud, her own throat, working.

You have to let him live a normal life, he said. He kissed her fingers, breathed out. Let it go. His eyes, she noticed, were shut.

Toxic Bonds surfaced in the Oxfam Shop. Its embossed silver title glittered across from the Fairtrade Coffee stand. On the cover, three short sentences, ranged like lines of poetry, sat beneath a cartoon heart. The heart was chained. Fear is Toxic. Clinging makes a Prison. Love means Letting Go. Embossed so they rose from the book's crimson background, these lines frazzled under the strip-light, sending a cold-water shiver down her neck.

Martha took the book home and read it the same night. It told her things she already knew, but with fewer caveats. A good mother was not driven by fear. A good mother did not limit the growth of what she loved. A good mother did not cling, for clinging was a curb upon joy. The good mother wished only to set free.

There were pages of exercises: mantras, deep breathing, checklists, a slew of limp phrases encouraging letting go. Spend today without consulting your watch and see what happens! Imagine a perfect beach, your child free from danger, playing separately in the sand! It was trite and predictable. It was embarrassing. But it was compulsive nonetheless. She went to the spare room in the small hours, sleepless, and read it all over again, this time marking it with highlighter pen. Near dawn, she dozed enough to imagine a huge animal with heavy paws had come in the room, strolled twice round the bed choosing its moment, then pounced, silent, onto the quilt to place its paws on her chest, pressing till she couldn't breathe. Even struggling to wake, she knew no beast was there. Of course not. Her eyes scanned for shadows in any case, so she unfocused her eyes, stared at nothing instead. Since the sound of her own breathing was frightening, she took the book's advice and spoke out loud. Let it go. The ghosts of passing cars travelled as lights along the ceiling cornice. Let it go. She had to understand what that meant. Let it go. There was no danger. No broken glass, lurking electric cables or razor-edged crockery. The beast in the dark was, and she knew it, only herself.

A trip to a counsellor recommended by a work friend of Riley's was not a success. The counsellor, a sad-eyed, unhealthily overweight single parent, offered chocolate biscuits. Martha had trouble meeting her eyes.

Do you do that on purpose? the counsellor said, creaking in her chair.

What? Martha asked.

That – detachment thing? You don't look as though you really want to be here.

Martha looked away again. The counsellor prodded Riley instead. That seemed more fruitful.

In the second session, Riley's Canadian origins declared themselves. He missed the open space, he said, its place in his heart. Some day, he'd go home. The word home did not mean their house: it meant the place his mother lived, the place from which she sent dried autumn leaves every year, pictures of her allotment.

Peter would love it there, he said. I did.

He tried for a smile, failed. The counsellor touched his hand. She liked Riley, Martha thought. Down-to-earth, reasonable-to-a-fault; everyone loved Riley. Her too. Maybe it was the easy-going suggestion of Irishness about his name. Her own made people think of Jesus and domesticity if they knew the biblical stories. These days, a lot of people didn't. Riley, as a name, seemed unlikely to date. At the end of the session, Martha handed over the suggested donation while Riley made a fresh appointment. After three, she called a halt. Riley asked what in god's name she thought they should do instead and Martha told him straight. His mouth fell open.

What do you mean, separate? You mean live apart?

Martha waited.

I thought we were trying to work together? I thought –

Divorce, Martha said. The words had come out no one else's mouth. I think I mean divorce.

The words surprised her, but only slightly. That was what separate usually meant: a cowardly, slow-death route to definite distance. She saw no reason not to call it by its name.

It's only fair, she said. I can't live with me either.

Riley was exasperated. There's no getting through to you any more. You're completely – he raked his mind for the right word – cut off. He kicked the skirting. What is it you actually want, Martha? Apart from endless fucking patience and permission to fall to pieces whenever you are overcome by the horror of normal life? What do you want?

She watched him struggle to regain control of whatever it was he was losing, looked at the square smudge on the wall, at a place where a picture had been taken away but had left its shape behind. She wondered what it had been a picture of. She did not say, I want to let you go. He would not have the faintest idea what she was talking about. I want you both to be safe. She barely understood it herself. The square on the wall seemed to pulse in the dim light.

I'm not leaving, he said suddenly. If that's the idea. I'm not going to be the one who packs his bags and strolls off into the sunset. He was indignant, his voice rising. I'm not abandoning anyone. It's not me.

No, she said, gathering herself. She kept her voice soft. It's not you. I didn't say it was.

Riley looked at her as though she had just stepped out of a human skin and shown a terrible, alien self. It was, she knew, the beginning of something unstoppable.

I won't ask for a thing, she said. Least of all Peter. She cleared her throat. I'm sorry. I'm not trying to hurt you. Either of you. It's me.

There was no bargaining or even shouting. He took it, Martha reported to her sister in Melbourne, on the chin.

White silence came down the line, a crackle of static.

Jesus, Sarah said. You can't just cut your own kid out like a tumour. Christsake, Martha, you're his mother.

I'm not cutting him out, Martha said. What's being cut out, if you must, is me. I'm – the word toxic skipped through Martha's head like a black lamb, disappeared – I'm a drain on him just now. Both of them.

She heard Sarah's intake of breath.

Don't talk to me as though I'm stupid, Martha pressed. Surely I need to acknowledge what I can't do?

There were a few seconds of nothing, of thick, under-water silence.

Martha. You know what Nancy always called you? Are you there?

Martha said nothing.

She called you her rock. Martha's such a bloody rock.

Martha looked at her nails. She should have washed her hands. Let it go, Sarah, she said. Trust me. I'm your sister. Make a leap of faith.

Jesus, Sarah said. Jesus H. Christ. Faith in what?

Martha heard her sister sniff, tried not to admit she might be weeping.

You really want out of it, don't you? That's what it means. You've had enough and you're cutting loose – is that it?

It's for Peter, Martha said, trying to keep anger out of her voice. And for the best.

Yes, I know, the phone said. It's for the best. Now where have I heard that before?

Sarah, you've no right—

As though topping herself did us all a favour. That was for the best according to that stupid bit of paper she sent. The back of a petrol receipt, if I remember correctly. And you got that. I got a fucking photocopy. Nothing personal, no apology. It's for the best. You can't even muster the gumption to be original, Martha. You've got this from her.

Martha held the phone tight. Nancy has nothing to do with it, she said slowly.

Not any more, she hasn't. But that's some legacy she left behind. You can't even see it, can you? *It's for the best.* She sounded drunk. Well thank god for that. Thank god for a catch-all get-out clause and good old mum.

Martha felt struck. What Nancy had done bore no comparison with her own situation. She could have reminded her sister that she, the youngest, had been the one left to deal with their mother's death; the shock, the police, the unanswerable letters; the one who, at seventeen, had arranged a funeral and dealt with the legal mess while Sarah sat tight in Australia, finalising her fucking wedding plans. But what was the point? Sarah had gone native. She swore all the time. All she knew was how to get on a high horse and ride into the distance.

Yes, Martha said. Thank god mum killed herself. Thank god for family.

Martha heard one of her nieces wailing in the background, needing attention. Sarah just held the line for a full thirty seconds. Then her voice creaked back down the line, dark, deliberate.

One thing, Martha. You're still a bitch.

The flat had white walls, a spare room and a fridge that made rock-fall noises at random intervals. Martha woke a lot in the night but that was to be expected. It was adjustment. She cried at the ceiling on and off for two days, then asked for tranquillisers from the new GP who asked very few questions. She needed full-time work to be occupied, and better useful, so supply was the obvious choice. High demand, nothing local, nothing permanent, nothing personal. No one paid much attention to who filled for a teacher off sick and not much attention was exactly what Martha wanted: no questions about family, what she did on weekends, just gratitude she had turned up at all. Supply was perfect.

*

From Peter's very first weekend with her, he brought photographs: Riley's idea. There was Peter sitting on a rug she did not recognise; eating breakfast from a familiar plate, but playing with an unfamiliar kitten on the old kitchen floor; reflected in the bedroom mirror, displaying his new school tie. Riley was showing he could fill the gap. They were good pictures, but curiously disquieting, and questions – does the kitten have a name? are those your new shoes? – irritated Peter enough for her to ask fewer as the months progressed. Riley did not phone. He needed the break to be clean, he said, to get his head around things. He hoped she would give him that. Martha understood. She understood completely.

After nine months, Riley had his head around all he needed. A handwritten letter, complete with a brochure of a trim little school and a photo of Martha's mother-in-law watering fruit bushes in her garden, said he wanted very much to go back to Canada. Peter would love having his grandmother there all day, the wide open spaces. Unless Martha wished to raise an application for sole custody, he hoped she would meet and talk it through, hear what he had to say. This was his new voice for her, between formal and informal. It was optimistic. It was strong. The terrible surge of tenderness and loss that rushed upon her at its close, at her husband's signature written more legibly that she'd ever seen it before, made her sit for a moment, compose herself, pour a drink. Surely he did not think she would object. She had put the most valuable thing in her life in his care already. That was the point. It was for her to adjust, Riley to do all the right things. Because he would. He always had. Her job now was not being difficult, or getting in the way.

She waited till evening before calling, then couldn't speak. He waited. Eventually, she read the important thing she had to say from the card she had written out before dialling, just in case. He was grateful. He hoped it would be a relief, in time; a way for her to have space. If she wanted to write, he would pass her letters on. His mother, he said, asked after her kindly. There was a catch in his throat for a moment, then a more familiar tone, the Riley she had lived with, came down the line.

I wish you could see the school, the voice said. They've got a jazz band, a mountain survival team, British-style soccer. And there's some kind of whizz-kid Art teacher who— Then he was silent. He was silent so long Martha thought he had gone. Eventually, the line crackled.

Well. It's a good place, he said. You get the picture.

The line was breaking up again. Not sure he could hear her, Martha said yes. Yes, she said, I do. Her words seemed to vanish into white noise.

Whatever's best, she shouted. Ellen is a wonderful woman.

Then Riley knew that already. It was a stupid thing to say.

Whatever you think, she called, hearing only an echo of herself. I know you'll do the right thing.

When all hope of Riley's voice resurfacing disappeared completely, she hung up.

*

For his last visit, Peter brought a drawing – a house in the woods with a wolf outside, the forwarding address and phone number in Riley's handwriting. Riley had used a ruler under his writing to keep it controlled, so the words were flat-bottomed, like little boats. Martha kept the visit routine; shared tv with a picnic on the rug, the park to see squirrels, colouring, what-if games. What if we could live on an island cooped up, safe. We'd find animals, Peter said, make friends. Routine things. Peter off-guard was what she wanted to remember. They watched a plane cross the clouds from the kitchen window, but he did not raise the subject of leaving. Provoking him to reveal his feelings, whatever they were, seemed crass. It mattered not to load Peter with emotions he didn't need, namely hers. For now, there he was, in the kitchen. She wished only to seize the moment, to drink him in.

After, she put the drawing with some family snaps, a left-behind jumper, and sketches her son had made, in a shoebox. She fished out a file of legal, household and financial stuff, not all of which she clearly understood, and set it alongside. Last, she foraged what Riley had always called that fucking casket – a black jewellery case, light enough to pass for empty – from the bottom of the wardrobe and settled it beside the rest. Her life – proofs of ownership, property, existence – done, dusted and not much when it came down to it. The half-bottle of cheap malt she had bought for emergencies (her mother's phrase) when she first moved in seemed justified. Tomorrow, she'd clear up, lock the papers away – in the airing cupboard maybe, beneath the bed. But not tonight. She couldn't do it tonight. Tonight was for sitting on the carpet beside inanimate objects, pouring till the bottle stopped delivering.

In the early hours, knees creaky, she wandered to the kitchen. The motorway lights made bright clusters. All day and all night, cars travelled this road. People went about their business with no let-up, driving. It was what people did. Sour fumes rose from the glass, nipping at her eyes. Peter was out of harm's way. She could not touch him, perhaps, but he was free from danger, open to joy.

All she had to do was bear it. I'm here, she said, watching the words fog on the window pane. And so she was. Still here. She stood till morning, forehead pressed against the window, watching cars on the slip road veering sharply for the fun of it, taking corners way too fast.

Martha wrote to Peter once a week, a recitation of school stuff, animal stories, fragments of silly conversations she had overheard. When he wanted, Peter wrote back. He developed a wild flourish under his name, more even handwriting, a talent for cartooning. Now and then, Riley enclosed a snap in which she could see her son's face changing; his hair turning longer, darker, blurring out his eyes. Insomnia apart, her own new life continued without much to remark upon. Supply teaching was steady and largely self-directed. She took poems into Chemistry classrooms, conducted debates on animal welfare in Physics, played Philip Glass in Maths and bet they couldn't count the notes. Few asked what she had done. They expected her to be on the sidelines. On one occasion, a shy Religious Studies teacher invited her on a field trip – an unrepeated adventure. On another, she joined a fourth-year trip to see *Romeo and Juliet*, astonished by the level of ready embarrassment sixteen-year-olds could muster. She was not part of the natural catchment for Retirement Dos and Nights Out. She went alone to concerts, leaving early if the music seeped too far beneath her skin. She experimented with photography, Modern Architecture and Ancient Greek at night-school till there was no space left in the week and she realised what was obvious. She preferred to be alone.

By Peter's twelfth birthday, the letters arrived once or twice a year: hers went weekly, as before. Afraid of email, horrified by the overfamiliarity of social media, she stuck with pen and paper, guessed his tolerance for it was fading. He was still recognisable from the pictures Riley sent on, had the makings of solid shoulders, astonishingly white North American teeth. That Riley accepted the money she still sent by wire made her grateful. What else did she have to give? Now and then, she wondered how she would respond if asked to visit, but no invitation came. On her fortieth, the small group who shared her lunchtime crossword surprised her. In tentative party mode, they cracked open a bottle of something fizzy and Grace from Home Economics made tray bakes. Fifteen more years and you can do what you like, she said, raising her glass for the toast. People made jokes about their ambition to be a former teacher one day. The age where life began, they said: she should make some plans. Tom, an Assistant Head with a thing for snazzy ties, gave her a gift: a coffee-table book, its cover showing Table Mountain, a palm-strewn beach, a scatter of ruins under a Turkish sky. 101 places to see before you die. General laughter. Everything worth seeing before you died was too far away, Martha said, and they laughed again, gave her an unaccountable round of applause. Life begins before you die – she saw the joke. Then her eyes became treacherous, her nose threatened to run. The wine, she thought, blinking; an unexpected act of kindness. Then the bell rang to remind her a class were waiting at the other end of the corridor. No rest for the wicked. No indeed. Everyone seemed relieved.

The class knew too – HAPPY BIRTHDAY chalked on the board in the hope of banter instead of lessons, and a cup-cake from the school shop studded with jellybeans.

Martha shelled out the extracts of Orwell she had brought for discussion, refusing to be deflected. She didn't like his stuff, but it was syllabus, an instruction from the absent teacher. Dutifully, she praised the author's tenac-ity, regretted the flatness of his characters, then asked for opinions. Fifth year concluded that Orwell was a creature of duty rather than passion. One, finding a photo on his phone, said Orwell looked repressed enough to implode.

His son almost drowned, Martha said. They looked at her.

They went out in a boat and were caught in a whirlpool. The little boy was only four years old, but Orwell took him into danger, then had to save him from drowning.

The class looked at her, then each other, wondering what point she was making. Martha had begun to wonder herself.

Sometimes, she said, there's more to people than meets the eye. Repressed and paranoid and dying is not a whole picture of anyone. Maybe he was passionate too. Maybe he was more passionate than he looks.

The boys hooted, pointing at his haircut, his stupid toothbrush moustache. Nobody in their right mind would ever fancy him – he had piggy eyes.

Martha was glad when the period was done.

The blood came and went for a year before she thought twice. The GP advised a hospital check, and Martha sat in the waiting room of the same building she had been with Peter all those years ago, thinking how terrified she had been. Not now. This was a fuss about nothing. The hospital noted her weight loss, nausea, spotting between periods. Only the sudden bursts of pain seemed unexpected. The probes and scrapes were not more bearable because they were the right thing to do, but they did not last long. When no one volunteered a cause she did not push. The word cancer popped into her head, and she let it, testing how it felt. She had been waiting for something, but illness had never been a fear. That ache in her spine that faded only when – if – she slept was no more than poor posture. More than likely, the care and time they were spending on her now was a waste of valuable NHS cash. On the other hand, the word cancer came back, flirting. She was, she understood, not frightened. An echo, some long-lost bird from another life entirely, seemed ready to fly home to roost.

Last day, Martha took her name off the supply list. There was no need to do anything else. Temps came and went: just the nod to the authority and she was a free woman. All this time at no one's beck and call, even a little room to extemporise, had been a good innings. Now there were other things to do, and she'd do them alone. They began with clearing: trousers that no longer fit, unloved dresses and unwise shoes, half-used cosmetics and never-opened books – things already overstocked at the charity shop. She gathered every set of class notes, minutes and reminders, keen to burn them in a fire-bucket to no more than ghosts. What was necessary to keep was not a great deal, when it came down to it. It occurred as she ransacked the cutlery drawer set on getting rid, she had not been this calm since late pregnancy. Maybe this was a kind of inversion, a clearance rather than the thing all those years ago they called nesting. It would have been amusing if she had felt less driven. Soon there was only the formal paperwork to go.

Her skin rippled at the spare room's habitual chill. Next to the bed and the hillock of newly-bagged rubbish, the cabinet – Martha's filing system, her cache of memorabilia – was still to go. It was important to leave things clean. Not to leave a mess behind. The things in the cabinet, if she remembered correctly, were by and large already shipshape. A few extras had been added over the years – bank-books, payslips, tedious financial stuff – but the essentials were as she had last settled them, nothing missing. The shoebox, however, should be opened.

The lid came back with a soft pop. Peter's jumper, tinier than she remembered, his drawings, the bright red NEW ADDRESS card showed all at once. Beneath them, snaps of Riley as a younger man, some Canadian dollars, tickets for a puppet show in Montreal. One shoe no bigger than the palm of her hand, its navy-blue leather gone dry as card. All to keep. She set the box aside. The green files full of birth and marriage, assets and confirmations, needed only the merest glance. Then the jewellery box. Without thinking nearly hard enough, she settled her thumbs on the gold-rimmed lid, lifted.

A waft of dust and velvet. Beneath a layer of crushed tissue paper, looking more frail than before, were the cuttings. The folded edges of the first cutout showed acid brown. Opened, however, the photo inside was exactly the same: its grey-dot composition sudden and familiar. The car. Some featureless, hired runabout, square in the middle of the frame, its tyres at a queer angle, half-sunk in mud. No marks on the bodywork, not a single scratch, showed. If it hadn't been for the shattered windscreen, its open shark-mouth gaping over the bonnet, you'd have no idea how terrible this was, none at all.

Slowly, Martha took in its details afresh, the nothing-much content of the photo refusing to change. A woman walking a dog had found it, they told her. A woman. Martha pictured an unsuspecting soul in a car-coat holding a lead, knuckles knocking gingerly on the window. Then she would look inside. When the paper began to shake in her hands, she set it down. What looked up from the casket now was her mother's face, young and wary and radiant all at the same time. Something in the quality of the photograph, the time of day, perhaps, made her quite ordinary set of features seem lit from within. Her mother in a garden, the leaves on the tree behind her wild with blossom, holding a baby, her firstborn, out to the watcher like a gift.

Martha settled her hand on the rug to settle herself and the cutting tipped her skin: the car, the mud, the broken-necked angle of the front tyres blatantly on show. Some godforsaken hillside in Cumbria, they said. Did they have a connection with that part of the country? Not so far as Martha knew. No suicide note either, not really; just four words on a petrol receipt, another razor blade (was it back-up?), a bottle of vodka and the car radio, on full blast till the battery gave out. After that, the stranger's problem; the stranger's burden to find the mess.

Overcome with shame, Martha pushed the clipping back

inside the box, her mother's picture with it. Trying not to think of blood gone black on cheap upholstery, she settled the lid then she stroked her skirt over her hips, again, again, making it smooth. She was not flustered. She was – what? Surprised. More than that. A fraud. Riley's voice whispered in her ears – *Get a grip, Martha. Throw that fucking casket away*. Like an arm around her shoulders. Good old Riley. *Get a grip, Martha*. He would always be there, true and clear, dispensing restraint and disappointment. *Get a grip*. She almost smiled.

The consultant repeated himself, asked if she understood. Martha nodded. Endometrial hyperplasia, a short presentation on overproduction of female hormones, thicknesses of some kind where they ought not to be, an overview of statistical probabilities. She had heard every word. Understanding would take a little longer. He smiled, spoke again. There was a very slim possibility of carcinoma, but it seemed as likely, in his opinion, as the present political class developing any interest whatsoever in proper handling of the NHS. He'd stick his neck out and say – he paused, looked her in the eye – it was wholly treatable.

Martha said nothing.

Given her age, he recommended hysterectomy, radio-therapy if any risk remained, but, insha'Allah – he smiled – complications were less rather than more likely.

There was a long, glutinous silence.

Perhaps he had been hoping she would be relieved and

was disappointed by her blankness. Maybe other people said things at times such as this, whatever kind of time it was. Martha, aware it was rude, found nothing.

Well, he said. A lot to take in.

He gave her leaflets and a prescription. The important thing to remember was that this was good news. He gave her a thumbs-up. Martha said nothing at all.

The front door looked shabby when she got back, in need of repainting; the brass lock tarnished. The key, however, worked first time. Maybe she had finally got the knack. For a while she stood at the kitchen window, wondering out of habit where the cars were going, not much caring. She spread her hands on the worktop, observed the tracery of veins and tendons under the skin. She put on the radio, found the shipping forecast, turned it back off. She made a cup of tea she didn't want, then wandered back to the balcony window. She could think of nothing, not a thing, she wanted to do. A walk maybe? The squirrel park with hazelnuts to attract company? Opening the balcony door let the sound of the motorway rush to meet her. Like opening a hive, she thought, a can of bees. The air was welcome, even if it stank of carbon emissions. It was cold. A gentle slap. Boxes and bags, the results of her former tidy-fit, made a ladder at the rail.

She had no desire to welcome any of it back. On top, however, was the unwieldy coffee-table book, its glossy colours pocked with rain. South Africa, the Maldives, the fallen city of Persepolis. 101 places to see before you die. If the wind had not flapped at the cover, she might not have seen inside it at all. But she did. Anticipating, as usual: your worst fault, Martha, is the way you shockproof yourself from surprise, the way you always need to know what's coming. The image of Canada she had made in her head, all autumn leaves and giant trees, did not show on the pages after all. The book had blown open, on not another continent, not even another country, but on Orwell's island. All by itself, the book chose Jura.

Two trains and a ferry; obligatory car hire, another boat. The cloud stayed low. Missing the second boat was a three-hour wait, inside the car near the water's edge, the island floating and not floating, hardly any distance away. At the other side, the deer were already waiting. Thirty for every human being on Jura; man, woman, child. The island was named for them and full of them, leaseholders of all they surveyed. The rightness of seeing them that first night called her every night thereafter with no need to find them out: they just arrived, in lines and clusters, family groups; now and then a solitary young male, chased away to make his own arrangements.

After a few days of simply watching without having to analyse a damn thing, Martha felt no pressing need to watch her step. No one intruded, no one demanded explanations. She spent the time taking pictures, sleeping a lot, identifying flowers and seaweed, shells, droppings.

She found things: a broken gate behind which a mob of pheasants gathered every night at dusk; the cemetery just outside Craighouse, its skulls and anchors, its flat-faced stones facing out so the dead might enjoy the view; a warehouse where the distillery stored its ancient casks, reeking of alcohol; a thicket of fat blue-black brambles. The territory was to be taken as found.

Her drive explored the single-track road a little longer each day, heading past the Highland cows and sheep that sat squarely, possessively, on the warmth of the tarmac. At night, she went out to whatever stretch of beach took her fancy, leaving the torch behind and picking her way by the low light that seemed to lurk always behind the dark. Now and then, the cry of a solitary raptor sounded from nowhere; a fox cub, keening. Other than that, only the sound of her own footfalls, waves – there were always waves – and wind, whipping at nothing. Her fingertips throbbed with cold. She inched out of the car near cliff drops, places where the road seemed almost to disappear over a sheer edge to the open sea; she rolled down the window for the pleasure of hearing the unseen blackness of tide beneath. I am perched, she thought, on the edge of the world. It was not frightening.

On her last evening, a passing-place she had not used before allowed her to leave the car and wade over boggy ground to a sheer fall of quartzite, a place to look out into the lighthouse flares, enjoy the sour hiss of the sea. Since the moon was high, the huge white breakers rising vertically beyond the safety of the strand showed clearly, standing upright before they melted like apparitions. For a second, she thought she saw a seal in the down-rush, but it might have been seaweed. Or nothing at all. Martha waited. She waited till she was too cold to wait any more, looking out at the battering wash, the rocks splintering whatever came into spray. There was no hidden code, no message, no meaning. What happened out there was random, wholly without blame or favour. In the end, nothing hinged on human decisions, nothing demanded retribution or just deserts: what happened was just what happened. She imagined Orwell in his stupid little boat, imagining he could spite the sea, getting away with it by chance. That boy. That terrified boy.

A stag made its low, calling bellow on the road behind her as she scrambled back to the car, leashing in the herd. Even this late, gulls were screaming at the tide. Everything seemed violently fresh, and she noticed for the first time a damp fog rolling closer, ready to blanket everything, even the webs in the hedgerows. Her jacket sleeve was already furred with droplets. Mushroom spores.

Godknew what was watching, its night vision clear, as she fought back to the car through blackness, her soles heavy with peat, but she knew it meant no harm. The night looked more dense when she flicked on the headlights, showing the mosquito net of water on the bonnet. Rather than turn, she chose to drive ahead a little further, find a side-track, then reverse: the single track made a clean turn

impossible. There was no rush. Martha wiped her eyes and
settled behind the wheel, her feet slipping on the pedals as
she clasped the belt. She turned the ignition, acknowledg-
ing the fact of it. It was time to go back.

The turn-off wasn't far. She backed into a clump of
heather, its hard roots scraping at the tail lights, made the
circle in three reverses. The way back was exactly that
which she had come. One road. It was still something to
come to terms with: this island had one road. Behind her,
if she had kept going, was Barnhill, the remotest place
on earth: after that, a petering out into broken scree, rock
and sweet FA. Ahead now were the settlements, the new
build, more fertile land, the tumble into Craighouse. Then
burned fenland, the road down to the sea. For company,
she pressed the radio button and found Mozart. It wasn't a
choice, just what came. Sometimes there was nothing but
white noise. It was a kind of miracle, finding Mozart first
time, some gorgeous voice at the top of its range singing
Queen of the Night. The singer's voice held no anger: it was
sheer, edgeless – a glass tower into the sky. The car dipped,
bouncing off a pot-hole and the firs closed ranks into the
downward slope. The world reduced to the headlamp
path, veils of drizzle on either side. A branch scraped the
window, making her flinch. She was driving too fast. This
road was poor in the best of weathers and here she was, not
behaving. She braked, cranked into second, felt the exhaust
scrape. It would help to turn the radio off. As she reached
for the dial to remove all distraction, the stag was already

turning. She caught a glimpse of his eye, his hooves, rising. Then the thud. Sudden. Grinding. Loud.

Instinctively, she pressed the brake, heard the sound of the engine dip. The car was ignoring her, making a slow-motion skid as if the bitumen beneath her tyres had turned to water. *Aquaplaning.* The word occurred as she tilted towards the passenger side, saw branches and distant lights panning past the window, vaguely aware she should release the brake. You were supposed to release the brake. Then, without apparent cause, without her doing the right thing at all, the car lurched to a stop. It took a moment for her to realise: it was facing the wrong direction. The Queen of the Night, shocking against the stillness, was still singing.

For a moment, Martha thought she saw something moving in the rear-view mirror, but it was just the nearside indicator, sending a signal, an absence, with no one to warn. Her neck hurt. But she wasn't dizzy. She was, to all intents and purposes, fine. Shaky, she sprang the seat belt and opened the door, scanned the horizon. She had hit some-thing, but what did not show. Not a rock fallen from one of the crags, it had absorbed too much impact for that. But something big. The stag. It had to be the stag. Able or not, it would have run. It would at least have tried. Carefully, tripping against the thick clumps of grass that forced their way up through the road surface, she walked to the rear of the car to check immediate damage, work out what to do.

The whole nearside wing was crushed, bent in on itself

like a worn slipper; one headlight pointing drunkenly into the trees. The radiator grille was squint. But no smell of petrol, nothing, apparently, leaking. At the bottom of the valley, a glowing window showed what was most likely a farm building, but it was too far to walk, too dangerous to leave the car like this. Someone else might come round the corner without warning, find the damn thing straight ahead. They might be on their way even now. A crow flapped from behind an open gate, the field beyond it thick as pitch. Then, by the steady, orange beats of the indicator light, she saw something move. Into the field and churned earth beyond the fencing, a beast struggling in a ditch. He was huge. He was desperate. He groaned, rose, fell back again.

Martha stepped over the ditch and onto the sodden peat, her stomach tightening. The beast, aware she was coming, kicked and tried to stand again, crashed heavily back down. She saw him rocking in the hollow, knees buckled, tilting his head and lowing. The shape of his antlers, small and new, flashed in outline against the fringe of rushes. There was no one else here. No one to help, no one to advise.

Trying for calm, she reached one hand, repeating what came into her mouth unbidden. I'm here. I'm here. Her touch against his flank made him shudder, and he twisted his head to see what she might be, eyes rolling white as he struggled, failed. A deep gash showed briefly under one of his back legs, and under his belly, something solid unfurling, glistening like oily rope. The iron smell of blood was unmistakable. This needed a gun. It needed a gamekeeper. She was too clueless to kill a living thing, could not imagine how. There would be a jack in the car maybe, but dear god. Not now. Not, she suspected, ever. She fought the sudden, awful desire to embrace the beast, wrap her arms around his neck and weep, but didn't. It would only make things worse, frighten him even more. And there, on the road behind her, was the car, a more-than-threatening hazard slant-wise on the single-track road while she looked on, spineless and stupid and out of place. Something slithered over the gate beside her, a hard black outline, claws scraping. All the time, the stag was shivering, heaving terrible, rancid breaths. She could not abandon him now.

I'm here, she said, reaching. Shhhh.

His back was thick, viscid; the bloody heat of him warm as soup. Kneeling on the grass, she felt rain seep through her jeans, spreading like shock. Gently, she placed her cheek against his flank, felt him flinch. His legs kicked instinctively, but their power was gone. Beneath her skin, however, his lungs pounded, ricocheting against her. He had no option but to fight.

Martha closed her eyes, leaned into him. This was all she had to give. She was Martha. A rock. She was forty-one years old. And despite herself, still here. Incapable of letting go.

Dislocated fragments of Mozart were gusting like feathers in the night air, ceding to an announcer who didn't belong here. Who had no idea what listened.

I'm here, she said, her words bouncing off the surrounding rocks and rising, furious, into the solid dark.

I'm here. I'm here.

acknowledgements

Publishers are shy of short stories in the here and now, shy like people are shy of three-legged puppies, which is to say they'd love to give them a home, but are nervous of their apparent handicap in that they are not novels. Since writing stories is something I'd hate to abandon, I am hugely grateful to Granta for taking them on and affording them to readers of the short form. I am indebted in so many ways. Thanks Bella and Pru and the team: you are a lifeline.

Further thanks to Jonathan for being my first reader and still my husband, to Alison for her constancy and to Hannah and the Dunbar Writers for being such wonderful company for this recluse on her trips out East to hear their work. You have been inspiring. The kindness of so many is something I am grateful for every day.

credits

Versions of the following stories in this collection have appeared elsewhere:

almost 1948 was commissioned by the BBC as a story to be broadcast on Radio 4.

fine day was commissioned by the Edinburgh International Book Festival and printed in an EIBF publication called *Lights off the Quay* with three other stories.

fittest was published by Oneworld Publications for *Beacons*, a collection of stories on global warming.

jellyfish was commissioned for *Headshook* (ed. Stuart Kelly), published by Hachette Scotland.

greek was screenprinted on top of photographs for *PhotoStories*, by Saatchi & Saatchi.

and drugs and rock and roll appeared as a very different version indeed in *Sex, Drugs, Rock'n'Roll: Stories to End the Century*, edited by Sarah LeFanu, published by Serpent's Tail.

Also by Janice Galloway and available from Granta Books
www.granta.com

THIS IS NOT ABOUT ME

'One of the most moving, yet completely unsentimental, accounts of growing up that you will ever read' *Scotsman*

With a boozy father, staunch mother and wild, domineering older sister, Janice Galloway grew up big-eyed and silent in Ayrshire, in a world where words and music were joyful secrets and domestic life veered between absurdity and dissolution. In this richly textured and darkly funny book, she evokes the hope and confusion of childhood, and describes how, slowly, the beginnings of unsuspected rage pushed a silent girl towards her voice.

'Her way of seeing has made her who she is, which is one of our finest contemporary writers, and this her most enjoyable, brave and telling book to date' *Sunday Herald*

'This is a dazzling book . . . Galloway is brilliant on the minute detail of childhood perception. She is also brave, funny, resilient and in spite of everything full of emotional generosity' *Daily Mail*

'A book unlike any other, in which Galloway has captured what it means to start to become yourself' *Guardian*

'Blistering, terrifying, always moving' *Independent on Sunday*

'Janice Galloway's fiercely moving book about her childhood in 1950s and 1960s Scotland is as far from a misery memoir as it's possible to imagine' *Metro*

ALL MADE UP

'A book unlike any other, in which Galloway has captured
what it means to start to become yourself' *Guardian*

In the second volume of her memoirs, the prize-winning
author Janice Galloway reveals how the awkward child
introduced in *This Is Not About Me* survived her teenage
years living with her stoical mother and domineering
older sister. In visceral descriptions of puberty, sex and
school-room politics, Galloway casts her extraordinary gaze
on the morals and ambitions of one small-town through the
stories of three generations of women.

'Galloway remains a brilliant writer, capturing mood and
character, time and place, with seeming effortlessness'
Guardian

'A fierce but forgiving tragi-comedy of manners, morality
and memory recovered' *The Times*

'*All Made Up*'s verbal playfulness, folksiness and wry,
hard-won humour are an antidote to the neurosis and
cynicism that can often characterise autobiographical
writing by the authors of fiction' *Independent on Sunday*

'Galloway is a mesmerising writer' *Scotland on Sunday*

'Janice Galloway is as good as they come' *Daily Telegraph*

'Warm, vivid, true' *The Times*

Keep in touch with
Granta Books:

Visit granta.com to discover more.

GRANTA